SHORT STORIES
Strange, Weird III
& Sci-Fi

Rich
DiSILVIO

Author's Website: www.richdisilvio.com

- - - - - - - - - - - - - - - - -

Names: DiSilvio, Rich
Title: Short Stories III: Strange, Weird & Sci-Fi / Rich DiSilvio
Description: New York, USA: DV Books, an imprint of Digital Vista, inc.
Identifiers: ISBN 978-0-9983375-8-6 (paperback) |
ISBN 978-0-9983375-9-3 (eBook)
Subjects: Short Stories | Mysteries, Thrillers | Sci-Fi, Fantasy | Artists, Composers
Illustrations/Photos: 16

THE AUTHOR

Rich DiSilvio is a multi-award winning author of thrillers, mysteries, historical fiction, Sci-Fi/fantasy, children's and nonfiction. He has written books, historical articles and commentaries for magazines and online resources. His passion for history, art, music, and architecture has yielded contributions in each discipline in his professional careers.

DiSilvio's work in the entertainment industry includes projects for historical documentaries, including James Cameron's *The Lost Tomb of Jesus, Killing Hitler, The War Zone* series, *Return to Kirkuk, Operation Valkyrie*, and cable TV shows and films such as *Tracey Ullman's State of the Union, Celebrity Mole, Blood Ties, Monty Python: Almost the Truth,* and many others.

He has written commentaries on the great composers (such as the top-rated Franz Liszt Site), and conceived and designed the Pantheon of Composers porcelain collection for the Metropolitan Opera, which also retailed throughout the USA and Europe.

His artwork and new media projects have graced the album covers and animated advertisements for numerous super-groups and celebrities, including, Pink Floyd, Yes, The Moody Blues, Cher, Madonna, Jay-Z, Willie Nelson, Miles Davis, the Rolling Stones, Alice Cooper, Queen, and many more.

As a software designer/developer, Rich pioneered the first interactive CD-ROM for educating staff and parents about Applied Behavioral Analysis (ABA) for training individuals with autism.

Rich lives in New York with his wife and has four children.

Contents

LIFE OF A SHYSTER

People call me a financial wizard, a money shark or, more often, a sly, no-good, filthy shyster. I make no bones about it; money drives me, always has, ever since my Bar Mitzvah.

My name is Jay Finkelstein. And yes, I was often called Rat Fink as a kid, so perhaps my lot in life was preordained. Anyhow, I guess the Bar Mitzvah ritual of becoming a man at age thirteen is not such a great idea; after all, thirteen is an unlucky number, right? I mean, Jesus—not that I believe in Jesus, nor in any other God—but mankind has branded thirteen as an unlucky number ever since its inception, when Judas Iscariot arrived late at the Last Supper. Hence, with Jesus sitting among eleven disciples, Judas was, you got it—guest number 13! *Oh, dear!*

That frightful number has been rejected or omitted by countless people for over two thousand years, even from elevators, as if the thirteenth floor of a building could somehow vanish without anyone noticing. So yes, stupid superstitions have shackled mankind since we learned how to walk on two legs. As I said, I'm a sly, shy...kind of guy. Well, okay, not shy, but you get the idea.

Anyhow, it was clear to me that money was *the* thing to have. After all, if Jesus beat my ancient ancestors out of the Temple because they were dirty dealers making money, then Hell, it had to be something compelling and great. After all, regardless of Christ's reprimands and directives, even Christians became perhaps the most money-hungry devils— popes, cardinals, and bishops included, who built huge, ostentatious cathedrals and still live amid lavish settings, while their poor flock scrapes together nickels and dimes to toss into their collection baskets.

Meanwhile, even though early Christians denounced bankers as sinful usurers they stayed in the fold with my kin, and, after many centuries, turned Wall Street into the Mecca of Money. So, don't kid yourself. Money *does* make the world go round, not prayers or blind faith, and without it, you're nothing. The tripe that living a clean, good life of moderation and giving regularly to the poor is a bowl of bison biscuits. And I don't care if you're Christian, Jewish, Muslim, Hindu, Buddhist or whatever. Because the global masses who have foolishly taken that avenue, believing that love and faith would be their sustenance, have crashed and burned, as debt, anxiety, conflicts, and the stress of money collectors hounding them turned their luminous spiritual fantasy into a life of misery, heartache, sickness, and even premature death.

Believe me, money *can* buy happiness. I know. I own a Learjet 45XR, a penthouse in Manhattan, a villa in Italy, an estate in the suburbs of London, a Rolls Royce, three Ferraris, and a Lamborghini Veneno Roadster; the Roadster alone cost me a cool four and a half million buckaroos. I know, I know—I'm a disgusting animal, a heathen, a fat, avaricious dirt bag, scum, a greedy pig, Rat Fink, and yadda, yadda, yadda! I get it. Jealousy from the little-minded masses has hounded me my whole life, like pilot fish clinging onto the great white money shark that I am. And I love being at the top of the food chain.

Okay, so I have a big ego, along with a very big waist from eating all the finest foods, prepared by the world's best chefs. But what did you expect? With big bucks and a big bank account comes a big head, and in my case, a big gut. They come as a package. Deal with it, or deal yourself a better set of cards, even if you have to cheat and steal a few aces and kings to stack the deck. You only live once, buster, so take it from me, go for it before your number is up. Yes, I played my winning hands, while often cheating, for over four decades. But remember, we *all* lose in the end. All of us. And I lost the big Game Of Life to the Big C.

Yes, all the money in the world is useless when certain forms of disease literally creep into your bones and eat you from the inside out. Just three days ago, my oncologist issued me the death-dealing cancer card. I was expecting him to hand me a Joker, but it turned out to be the Grim Reaper. *No Joke*. It was a shocker, all right. But you see, if I had lived a crappy, useless life of perpetually struggling to put food on the table or just to pay my bills, I would be bawling like a baby right now. But alas, I can hold my head up high. After all, I devised a new mantra that I tell my friends and relatives:

Seasons don't fear the Reaper. Nor do the wind, the sun or the rain; we can be like they are. Come on, baby. Don't fear the Reaper.

Pretty poetic, huh? Okay, I cheated and stole that, too, from some Blue fishy Cult, but that's the gist of it. I lived a great life, and have no regrets. But I've wasted enough time.

With only two weeks left to live, I need to be judicious on how I spend my time. As such, I couldn't leave this planet without paying a visit to my dear buddy, actually my young protégé, who helped me accrue my vast fortune, which is estimated to be roughly eight hundred and sixty million dollars. In truth, even I've lost count at this point. After awhile, even a nefarious numerologist like myself gets tired of counting.

But my skinny little buddy took good care of my estate and will. So, I decided that today I would visit James from the swamp. No, no, James Van Der Veen doesn't truly come from the swamp. You see, his last name in Dutch means *from the swamp*. Anyhow, James lives in the Netherlands, and being a low-key, down-to-earth sort of guy, James enjoys mingling with the lowly peasants in pubs. I suppose it's his way of paying tribute to his roots. But make no mistake; in the financial world, James is like a croc from the swamp—he's deadly and financially well fed, even if no one would ever know he's a millionaire.

I flew to the Netherlands and had my chauffeur drop me off near The Hague at the *Sherlock Holmes Bar*. Good old James, he knows I'm a Sherlock Holmes aficionado, having read Sir Doyle's books and seen all of the movies, from the first silent flick in 1916 with William Gillette to Basil Rathbone's rendition and right up to Robert Downey Jr. and Benedict Cumberbatch. Like a true Sherlock shyster, I learned at an early age how to deduce the best investments to gamble on and how to cleverly finagle my way to success with a cool, detached bearing, never giving in to emotion, at least while dealing in the financial arena. Okay, so I put a sinister spin on the Sherlock persona, but it paid off, literally.

So this Holmesy pub it is, with its nice little mural on the wall of Sherlock and Watson in their living room by the fireplace and Sherlock's trusty library nearby. While overhead, flags of different nations are tacked by their four corners to the ceiling and billowing, as if the winds of heaven are blowing the sails of a united league of nations toward some utopian shoreline of multicultural equality and financial equity. A delusion on all accounts, I must say.

So here I now sit, downing a dark and disgusting Guinness with my one, true-blue pal, whose lanky body is decked out in a pink Izod shirt and torn Levis.

"James, how the hell can you drink this muddy water? I'd much rather have a Salvatore's Legacy at the *Playboy Club* in London."

As I swipe the frothy foam from my lips, James rolls his eyes. "You're such a highfalutin ass! You'd rather spend nine grand for one stinking drink than have nine hundred brews? You're an insult to all intelligent Jews!"

As I chuckle, the dark ale surges up my aquiline nose, which somehow turns into an atomizer as it sprays out a fine vapor. As James recoils from my nasal brew-mist, I catch my breath and say, "James, as a financial kingpin, you should know that owning one original Vermeer is better than seven hundred Polaroids of a Pollack. As you're aware, Salvatore Calabrese's famous drink utilized some of the oldest bottles available, like a 1788 Clos de Griffier Vieux Cognac, Dubb orange curaçao from the 1860s, and a shot of 1770 Kummel Liqueur. So instead of drinking a poor man's *Guinness* beer, I'd much rather have Salvatore's Legacy, which earned a *Guinness* World Record." Pushing the lowly pint of piss away, I add, "Jesus, Van Der Veen, I taught you how to make millions, but I could never expunge the grunge out of you. You even prance around in a crappy Izod polo when you could at least sport a Fred Perry. And pink? Seriously? You have no balls or class."

James shakes his head. "So you're going to be a pompous fool right up to the end, is that it? No remorse, no wisdom gained, no repenting for all your sins?" James slams his beer down on the table as his face turns into a snarl, one I had never seen before, as he continues, "Listen, Jay, I don't give a crap about your snob-nosed sense of class, because it's *you* who has his head up his ass. The fact is, your sickness has made me do some soul searching—and health screening—and I now know I'm probably not too far behind you. For your information, I probably already have one foot in the grave. I have prostate cancer, Jay, and although they tell me it *might* be curable, I know it's a signpost, just like the one Rod Serling talked about. You know, 'that's the signpost up ahead—your next stop, the Twilight Zone!'"

I would have nostril-sprayed James again if I'd been drinking, but instead I hold back the laughter and offer him a paternal reply. "James, you're losing it. Christ, you don't even know how bad your condition is and you're already jumping overboard, abandoning your ship. You're a shitty captain, James. Shut up and stay the course, like I've shown you all your lowly, pathetic life. I taught you how to make millions, yet you've chosen to live like a pauper." Turning around, I gaze at all the middle-aged trash hanging out at the bar with their stupid, childish T-shirts and scruffy faces peering up at the flat screen TVs, only to watch more overgrown idiots kicking a stupid ball around, I snicker and gaze back at my young, foolish chum, or rather, *chump*. "You know, I came here to spend some quality time with you, James, since *I'm* the one on death row. But here it seems you expect *me* to console and coddle *you*. Grow up! Before you make me throw up!"

James squints as his blue eyes intensify with rage. "Well, get this, Mr. Macho Money-man, who thinks he's so damn smart. I asked you here for a reason, and it wasn't to extract pity. It's to tell you how I've extracted your fortune, right out from under your big, arrogant nose!" As my eyes squint with indignation, he goes on, "You entrusted me to be your executor and to distribute your wealth to, of all things, your various millionaires clubs, which are disgustingly overfunded already by all your rich friends. Correction, you have no friends. They all despise you, just like your wife and entire family that abandoned you. Even your long string of mistresses left you. You're a crass, egotistical, fat pariah." Pointing at the people in the bar, James continues his charge. "You may mock and belittle these people, but they have hearts and souls, something you never had. The only faces that will appear at your shiva are those of Ben Franklin, Hamilton, Jackson and the like. And your legacy will be just like those flimsy bills, cheap paper that will dissolve over time, as there's nothing solid and golden about *you*!"

My nostrils flare as I reach over the table and grab his effeminate wrist. "Never mind your self-righteous bullshit, Twinkie. What do you mean you extracted my fortune?"

But before James could even respond, two large men edge their way to our table as one pulls out a Glock 43, and sticks it in my face. "You're the piece of shit that screwed my boss. Don't make a scene, Finkel-face, or I'll blow that ugly thing right off your shoulders. Got it, tubby?"

Meanwhile, the goon's buddy grabs James by the neck and pulls him up to his feet. "And you're this fat fink's fruity accomplice, Van Der Queen. You'll be coming along with us, too!"

James's face twists with indignation. "First of all, you homophobic nitwit, great men like Michelangelo and Tchaikovsky were gay, men that a slimy slug like *you* could never match, or even understand."

At that, the brute smacks James hard across the face. Shaken, James wipes his bloody lip and asks, "Okay, okay, s-so whom are you w-working for? We'll gladly pay you more, if you just—"

The thug gut-punches James, who keels over with a guttural moan, but is pulled upright again by the thug's other hand, which is still firmly clasped around James's frail neck.

My goon slips his Glock into his jacket pocket, still pointing it at me, and says in a menacing whisper, "Enough of the silly games. Head toward the door, fatty, nice and casual-like." With a jiggle of the pistol in his pocket, he adds, "Or else I'll get a chance to use my nine-millimeter on you."

I couldn't resist. "I figured your *little* pistol to be only nine-millimeters."

My head snaps back as his lightning-fast fist pummels my mouth and retracts before I can even blink. "Ughh!" I bellow, as he grabs a napkin off our table and pushes it against my bloody lips. "There you go, sweetheart. Keep it up, and I'll show you the girth of my pistol in ways that will truly make your head snap back. Now, shut up and get your fat ass moving out the door, quietly!"

I certainly was never a macho kind of guy, especially being five-foot-six with a mostly bald head and squinty eyes clad with glasses, all while weighing in at two hundred and thirty pounds, but when you only have two weeks left to live, it sort of gives even fat wimps like me a shot of testosterone. With a smartass look, I say, "Hey, dickhead, in case you haven't heard, I only have two weeks left on this shitty planet, so spare me your dumb gorilla gab." as I wipe my bloody lip, I add, "And the cheap pussy shot."

With a firm slap to the back of my head, he says, "Shut your yap, fatty, or I'll punch your teeth down your throat, all the way to your fat ass. Then again, since you're already talking out of your ass, I see someone beat me to it."

Grabbing my tie, he yanks it, then drags me like a dog on a leash through the crowd. As I choke and practically trip over my stumbling feet, I say with a gasp, "So I take it you no longer care about making a scene?"

Without a word, the gorilla continues to plow through the crowd with his free hand while a crazy idea enters my head. Spontaneously, I reach into his pocket and pull out his Glock just as we exit the bar. Sticking it into his massive back, I say, "Okay, Magilla, let go of my tie before you get a piece of lead in your hairy back."

Swiveling around, his eyes widen, but the real surprise is that the other thug clocks me from behind, forcing me to drop the Glock as I grasp my swollen ear. As the gorilla attempts to retrieve his pistol, I swiftly kick it away and make a mad dash for a parked moped, which is idling while its owner is making a delivery. Hopping on, I floor it as I hear shots ring out at my back. Turning my head around, I gratuitously flip the gorilla the bird, only to see him rip a bicyclist off his ten-speed, hop on, and start peddling after me with fury in his apish face and the godly speed of Mercury in his feet.

Speeding down the narrow, brick-herringboned street of Balistraat, I pass a series of small shops while periodically peering backward. To my dismay, the Glocked gorilla manages to maintain a close tail on me, his ugly face red and gnarling with anger. I then turn onto the fashionable street of Lange Voorhout, and before long I pass the *Hotel Des Indes* on my right. Veering left at the fork, I travel into an open park with trees, when, out of the corner of my left eye, I spot the Lange Voorhout Palace. With the gorilla still on my heels, I turn and come to a halt. Standing before me is the entrance to the palace. Designed in 1760 by the architect Pieter de Swart, it had subsequently been turned into the Escher Museum.

Hopping off, I run inside so fast that I slip and slide right into a column and fall over. After a brief moment, I get up and run headlong into a crazy house of stairs. Befuddled, I dash up one set of stairs, only to find myself passing a series of M.C. Escher's lithographs on the walls. They're the weirdest images imaginable, yet endlessly fascinating, as I see optical illusions of fish morphing into birds, black horsemen facing white horsemen, each interlocked with no foreground or background between them, and all sorts of crazy, but ingenious, illusions. I don't know *what* ran through this man's head, but now *I'm* running through it! Suddenly, I adopt James's paranoia: *This stop, the Twilight Zone!*

Running up and down flights of stairs, I finally come upon an old monk, who beckons me to come closer. Overcome with exhaustion, I peer back over my shoulder, yet see no gorilla in sight. With a sigh, I turn around and march my fat body over to the monk, wheezing.

"My son, what ails you?" he asks. "You're running away from someone or something. Is there anything I can do to help you?"

Catching my breath, I once again glance anxiously behind me, then look straight into the old monk's hazel eyes. "What makes you say that?"

The monk chuckles. "My son, it is as clear as the rather large nose on your face. No disrespect intended, I merely state facts. But, you see, my vocation has placed me in the company of many souls in need of solace, empathy, or absolution. And being a very good judge of character, I can see you may need the latter."

I remove my glasses and begin rubbing them clean on my shirt as I squint my eyes, attempting to judge *him*. I peer around to see if someone put this man up to this, but find only the bizarre world of illusions around me. However, my eyes briefly fall upon a harrowing signpost, which jolts me. There, before my eyes, is Escher's haunting illustration of an eye with a skull lurking in the blackness of the pupil, reminding me of my own imminent death.

Gazing back at the amiable old monk, my mind suddenly recalls James's pointed remark: So you're going to be a pompous fool right up to the end, is that it? No remorse, no wisdom gained, no repenting for all your sins?

Suddenly I think, *damn, the sleazy bum may have stolen my fortune, but he had a point.*

Meanwhile, the pleasant monk awakens me from my musings as he says, "Well, son?"

Blinking hard, I eradicate my thoughts and peer back into his alluring eyes, eyes that look like those of a twenty year old, while he most certainly must be in his late seventies or early eighties. Added to his spellbinding eyes is his genial smile that has some sort of a lofty glow to it, as if this spiritual encounter was preordained.

Despite not buying into this whole spiritual awakening shtick, I must admit, this merry monk's celestial smile, purity of soul, and affable disposition can *almost* make *me*—a self-confessed sinner and proud atheist—a believer. With a shake of my head, I reply, "Father, uh, do I call you Father or Mr. Monk, or…it's not Adrian, by any chance, is it?"

The monk giggles as he clips his rosary beads onto his belt. "No, my son, I'm a bit too old to be Adrian Monk. But, Father would be fine. So, is it absolution you seek?"

"Absolutely! Absolution," I say with a smile, figuring I might as well have some fun in my last few days. And what better fun can there be than a Jew-turned-atheist pretending to be a Catholic?

The monk nods. "Very well, and what is your name, my son?"

I pause but a moment, and say, "Salvezza. Uh, Thomas Salvezza."

The monk squints. "*Salvezza*? That means 'salvation' in Italian."

Feigning surprise, I shake my head. "No? Certainly, you jest, Father. My parents never mentioned that. Are you sure?"

"Oh, yes, quite sure," he replies with a smile. "It appears fate has led you here today, Thomas, for the gift of salvation."

"Yes, a gift. I like gifts. And fate indeed, Father. You see, I suppose I do need salvation, as I only have two weeks to live. Cancer."

The monk's jovial expression withers to a solemn stare. "My, my. I'm grieved to hear that, Thomas. Would you like to confess your sins? It would be my honor."

Peering behind me, seeing no sign of the gorilla, then looking back, I was about to speak when a terrible pain pierces my chest, like a skewer to the heart. Clutching my chest with a cringe, I close my eyes and grit my teeth, as the monk swiftly grabs my shoulder and escorts me to a couch, where he lays me down. Fetching a glass of water, he returns and lifts my head. "Here, Thomas, take a sip."

As a bright, white light flashes before my eyes, the sudden fear of death grips me tight as I struggle to breathe. To my utter horror, I'm caught off guard. All along I've been facing this moment with a firm bearing, yet quite oddly, now that death is prematurely thrust upon me, a terrible fright surges through my veins, as if my blood was scorched by the devil and now boiling me from the inside out. As sweat beads up on my bald head, the monk tenderly grasps a cloth and pats it clean. "My son, you're burning up. Perhaps I should call an ambulance?"

"No, no. Please," I beg. "I don't want to die in some cold hospital room with IV tubes stuck in my arm and oxygen tubes up my nose. As you said, Father, it truly seems as though fate brought me to this bizarre world of illusion with you for a reason."

Drinking the water and taking deep breaths, I finally regain my bearings after several minutes, as my anxiety evaporates and my mind reaffirms the man I truly am.

Despite regaining my strength, I can't help this feeling of disgust with myself that permeates my mind. I've often heard the faithful deriding how atheists will buckle when the time comes, chiding, *"I'll be prepared when you're lonely and scared at the end of our days."*

Actually, that was Black Sabbath who said that, but the hell with that. I made my decision a long time ago, and could never buy into that childish illusion. Just then, my eyes catch a glimpse of another one of Escher's illusions nearby, this one being *Paradise*, with Adam and Eve. But this crazy Twilight Zone I'm in won't deter me. It's the religious fools who are weak. Like overgrown children, they need security blankets: to believe in a heavenly afterlife of peace and joy, since the mere thought of rotting away into an eternal abyss of nothingness frightens the hell out of them.

Gazing up at the monk, I say, "I'm ready, good Father, to confess my sins." With an internal giggle, I plan on giving this preacher of lies a good run for his money, something he surely never had to earn. Feigning remorse, I add, "But I fear there is no absolution for me, Father. So perhaps confessing my sins will all be in vain."

"Nonsense, Thomas. There have been many cases of men living sinful lives and being absolved. Even Saint Augustine lived a wayward, hedonistic life as a youth, only to become a bishop and a religious icon. It's a matter of *genuine* repentance or false testimony that governs the Lord's actions, acts of either clemency or damnation."

"*Damnation!* Dear Lord," I say with an impressive touch of frightful melodrama. "That's a very powerful and wicked decision. Is it not, Father?"

"Well, yes, a powerful decision by the all-powerful God in Heaven, Thomas. That is why we humans must not judge others, as those decisions reside with God alone."

I laugh inside. I have this *monk*-ey right where I want him. "So how then, good Father, do you explain our justice system? Court judges have the supreme power to set defendants free, or send them to prison, or even death row— sometimes even condemning innocent people to death in error."

The monk becomes fidgety as he runs his old, bent finger around his brown woolen collar. "Well, Thomas, mankind does many things in an attempt to mimic God and His divine rules, but we mortals are flawed, *all* of us. So, there's no need to dwell upon such things, especially now at this late hour of your life. I'm here to help you gain access to His holy realm. So, my son, I must ask. How long has it been since your last confession?"

My internal laugh is almost deafening as I fight to stifle my lips from revealing the farce. After a brief moment, I regain my composure and respond, "Father, I'm ashamed to even admit this, especially since I've been a devout Catholic ever since I was blessed in the waters of Baptism. I've gone to confession and received communion religiously every week, not missing a beat. But ever since my oncologist told me of my imminent death, I've failed to confess my sins. I've been a tainted man, Father, for weeks."

The monk sits beside me and pulls out his Bible. Placing it on his lap with his left hand firmly on its gilded cover and his right hand grasping my arm, he says, "Thomas, it is only recently that you have heard of this devastating news, so surely God understands. We humans do not always comprehend why or when He summons His children to Heaven, but distressing circumstances like this always warrant special waivers. So have no fear. God does not judge you in this case, and nor can I administer penance for something that is completely reasonable."

Again, I stifle a chuckle, realizing how strict creeds of *all* religions have been broken with lame excuses from the day they were written on papyrus. Why have rules if they can be broken and have no consequences? Yet, having lived a wayward life of sin, at least according to the Good Book, I truly believe there is no better way to end my wonderful life than to be stricken with a bad heart and cancer on this makeshift deathbed with a hapless monk, who's about to be shafted by the world's richest and most devious shyster.

Caressing my arm, the monk says softly, "And, please, take no offense, Thomas, but I'm bound by my vows to ask you: Have you ever fallen prey to gluttony?"

Now I had to laugh, as I bluster, "Well, just look at me, Father! I told you I have sinned. There can be no redemption for a blubbery walrus like me, now can there?"

As the monk covers his mouth to stifle a giggle, I contract my cheerful cheeks, turning them into droopy jowls of dejection, as I solemnly continue, "Yes, Father, I'm terribly ashamed. I have obviously lost my way." Bowing my head, I gaze somberly at the floor, projecting a fine image of disgrace and regret. Then, peering up with puppy dog eyes, I say, "But know this, Father—my whole life, I had always abstained from overindulging. Having been a Division One athlete in my college days, I maintained and honored my body as a sacred temple, eating in moderation and caring for my health and soul, by cleansing it weekly with purified water and receiving the Host for communion every Sunday." Honing my acting skills further, I manage to conjure up a tear of shame in my eye, as I gaze into his gullible eyes. "But when the good Lord authorized the doctor to deliver my death sentence, it weakened my constitution. I fell apart. I fell, I f-fell from g-grace." With my lips quivering, I close my eyes as the tear breaks free and courses down my plump cheek. Doing a swell job of feigning a whimper, I add, "I'm weak, Father. I deserve to be punished." I open my eyes and wipe away the tear. "Look at me, Father, and at what I've become. I lost my hair, my eyesight, and my once fit body to become this fat, unsightly blob. I'm a disgrace, unworthy of the Lord's love and grace."

"Oh, Thomas, that, too, is something there can be no punishment for." Placing his hand compassionately on my shoulder, he continues, "Your situation is one prone to abandoning all of one's senses and better judgments, so fear not. The Lord does not expect each and every one of His children to be like the other. We all take different paths to the Lord's Kingdom in Heaven." Patting my thigh, he adds, "Buck up, purge those silly thoughts, and let's move on, shall we?" Taking a moment, the monk gazes up at the ceiling, which may have been the floor, and then peers down at me and asks, "So, Thomas, have you ever given in to the sin of lust?"

Visions of all the women I had banged over the years suddenly come flowing back into my mind's licentious eye. In this I have no illusions: the allure of my millions had drawn women to ugly ol' me like flies to dung. Yes, money has the power to make even fat, repulsive men like *me* attractive. And boy am I glad that I loved to lust women. I wouldn't give up those lustful memories for all the gold in the world.

"Oh, Father," I reply with the tender and unripe voice of a virgin, "I am proud to say *never*. The mere thought of it makes my skin crawl, as the only physical union between a man and woman should be in the spiritual embrace of marriage, ordained by the good Lord above. And I have never had the good fortune of being married."

A miraculous grin enlivens the monk's face as he pats my chest. "Good man, Thomas. For a man not of the cloth to hold such a vow of celibacy is highly admirable. Underneath your initial impression of a man on the run, I sensed you were a pure and good soul. However," he says as he gazes at my wrist. "I see you're wearing an expensive Rolex, and this leads to my next question. Have you ever engaged in the sin of greed?"

"Dear Lord, *no!*" I say as I sit up in a dramatic display of genuine sincerity, so much so that I almost fool myself. "Yes, I am a very wealthy man, as you can plainly see, but I have donated the lion's share of my profits to various Chabads and JCCs..." Noticing the monk's expression, I realize I was mentioning only Jewish charities. To correct my foolish *faux pas*, I begin adding a host of Catholic and secular charities, to the monk's delight.

The monk, once again, pats my shoulder with a reverent grin. "You're a model citizen and true son of God, Thomas. And may I say, your doubts of not being forgiven are ill founded. Like your namesake, perhaps it's only natural that you're a doubting Thomas."

Again, I chuckle inside. Doubting Thomas, my ass! I'm a duplicitous Jay Finkelstein, Mr. Monk. And you're surely no Adrian Monk, as he would have discovered my charade long ago. But Hell, this silly old monk had said God absolves long-time sinners if they're genuine. And I'm *genuinely* having a ball now, so perhaps those pearly gates will open up for this former Jew and diehard atheist, and I can begin to climb that Stairway to Heaven that Led Zeppelin got so much praise and *money* for. Even though I'd much rather have *a new car, caviar, four-star daydream.* Hell, *think I'll buy me a football team.*

What can I say; *money, it's a gas.* Even Floyd knew that. And as for all the parasites that clung onto me only for my money, I say this: Not only will I miss the money more than them, but how is it that *they* never get chided the way we millionaires do? Just because we're in the spotlight doesn't mean Lucifer should roast only our hides. All the little cockroaches, snakes, and leeches also deserve to be scorched in the fiery flames of Hell.

After all, fair is fair.

But enough of this nonsense, it's time to see what else

this naive monk wishes to ask mawkish ol' me. "So, Father, do you think I'll make the grade? Of God's grace, that is."

The monk flips open his Bible, scans a few pages, then pauses. Reading a few lines, he then looks at me. "You're doing fantastically well, Thomas. I'm proud of you. I'd say you're an 'A' student. 'A' for Angel, of course." Chuckling at his own witticism, the monk then stares deep into my eyes. "But I just have two more questions, then you'll be as good as golden." Pausing briefly, he then says with a calm, steady voice, "Have you ever let anger steer you into sin?"

Still sitting upright on the couch, I rub my chubby chin as my shoulders wilt. "Well, Father, for a man like me, that's a very hard sin not to commit. So I must tell you, I often grow *very* angry." The monk's eyelids snap open as he leans backward and crosses his arms, awaiting the bad news.

Gritting my teeth, I say, "My blood *boils* with anger when I see men and women in bars, cursing and acting in disgustingly profane ways, or watching filthy television shows that break almost every rule of decency while ignoring God's righteous Commandments, as well as frittering away precious moments that could be utilized in prayer. So, yes, Father, *anger* consumes my very soul, intensely." Lowering my head in shame, I speak down, down toward the fires of Hell beneath the floor, where—according to the Bible—my soul should go. "So, as I forewarned you, Father, there can be no place in God's calm and dignified Heaven for an enraged sinner like *me*, now can there?"

The monk glances down at his Bible, once again. "My son, you never cease to amaze me. You have proven thus far to be a resplendent child of the Lord. Your anger, Thomas, is righteous anger, for those lost souls are the ones condemning themselves into a world of misery and woe. Anger of that sort is to be applauded, for as you say, such degradation and unseemly acts of sin even cause *me* much anger." Clenching his hand into a fist and shaking his head adamantly, he says, "So in no way, my child, could I ever administer penance for *that*, or any other confession you've made thus far." Taking a deep breath, the monk regains his lofty air of spiritual contentment, and says, "That brings me to the final question, Thomas."

As a big, pseudo grin graces my fleshy face, he says, "Have you ever deceived anyone?"

My eyes bulge and face blanches, as if a freight train were about to plow into me! In shock, my jaw drops. My seasoned poker face was caught off guard as I begin to stammer, "Uh, well, um, actually, F-father, I guess I have."

To my horror, before my very eyes, the monk's body contorts, twisting into the fiery red image of Satan! With curly black hair, a goatee, and two horns that sprout out of his head, he reveals a sinister smile with fangs like a velociraptor. Meanwhile, the Bible in his hand bursts into flames as his large, red claws grab me tight—one on my arm, the other around my flabby neck—as he spits a venomous scolding with his foul, fiery breath that could melt steel. "You slimy, deceitful fool! Did you really think a fat piece of shit like *you* could fool a devout monk?"

As I gasp for air and feel my heart burning with fear, Satan continues, "I enjoyed watching how far you attempted to take your stupid charade, Jay, but here's the deal. You're mine now, for all eternity. And just as you deceived others, I will continue to deceive you. Henceforth, I will make you suffer the heartache and pain that you subjected all of your poor, bankrupt clients to, by giving *you* a heart attack!"

With that, my heart begins to convulse. The excruciating pain and agony hurls me into a violent seizure as I fall to the floor, clutching my chest. With a harrowing shriek that could break glass, I scream as my heart bursts like a red balloon. The world goes *dead* black.

Jump-started like a car, my eyes open once again,

only to see Satan standing before me, a terrifying grin etched deep into his evil, wrinkled face, like incisions on a bloody cadaver. Crossing his muscular arms, he spreads his hairy, ox-like legs, and says, "One down, Fink, all of eternity to go!"

"*No!* No way!" I cry. "This can't be, this is bullshit!"

The demonic, inversed-Minotaur laughs. "Oh, I have plenty of deceitful tricks to play on you, fat Fink. Some may even include you eating brownies that turn into bull *shit*. Others may have you lustfully chasing beautiful women, as you did in life, only to discover in the midst of passion that you're sucking face with a blubbery-snouted elephant seal, or in honor of today's jest, an ugly monkfish!"

Struggling to get back up to my feet, I make a mad dash toward the Escheresque set of stairs. Running up, then down, then around again, I realize I've been inside an Escher illusion the whole time as my own body gradually morphs into an alligator, mimicking an Escher lithograph. Hearing a thunderous clatter of hooves coming up behind me, I turn to see Satan bearing down on me, his half-man, half-animal body causing my heart to flutter once again. In his clawed right hand is a pitchfork, the other a gnarly club with spikes. Having grown into a twenty-foot tall monstrosity, Satan snarls as he raises his weapons with ominous intent.

In utter fear, I cower and begin to weep. "Dear God, *no! Please!*"

"It's too late for that, Fink!" Satan blusters. With a powerful thrust, his two weapons hammer down on my alligator skull, cracking it wide open! *Death*, once again.

The painful nightmare continues 666 more times, as Satan inflicts one horror after another, with each one of my deaths more brutal than the former, as I experience the true meaning of Hell.

Jump-started like a *dead* old car, my eyes spring open once again. Only this time, the illusionary, Escheresque world of terror and suffering is gone. With a sigh, I gaze up, only to see the column in the museum lobby that I had slid into when I first arrived.

With my eyes beginning to regain their focus, I now notice a crowd of people hovering over me, one being a doctor, who bends down and says, "You've been knocked out for a good twenty minutes, mister. An ambulance is on the way; you very likely had a concussion. I strongly suggest we do a CT scan to be sure."

Sitting up, I rub my head as the lobby of the museum comes into full focus. "Dear God. No. Please."

"You already said that," the doctor says. "You had also been mumbling a few confessions these last few minutes, before you regained consciousness. From the sounds of those confessions, you seem like a very religious man."

"Dear Lord, no. *No*, I'm *not*, doctor. But if I can manage to get my fortune back from my deceitful friend, I intend to rectify my sins."

My eyes suddenly notice the gorilla standing by the door amid a growing throng of spectators crowding around me. With a shake of his head, the thug turns and exits, while passing him on his way in is none other than James, the slimy slug from the swamp, who approaches me. With a disgusted look on his face, he says, "I managed to pay off that other goon and followed you. Although I despise all the unscrupulous things you did in your rotten life, Jay, I came here to say, I've changed my mind. Let God do with you what he will. I'm washing my hands clean of you and your money, as well as this crummy profession of making money off the backs of hard-working saps. We're nothing but usurers, Jay. Sinful usurers. We produce *nothing*. We push around hedge fund papers and make millions while fleecing countless clients in the process. I'm done!"

As I stand up, I say, "I'm glad to hear you say that, James. I was just about to tell you that I want to change my will. I wish to donate my millions to various *real* charities, and—get this, James—I've decided to establish my own college. But not one dedicated to finance. Instead, one dedicated to the sciences, hi-tech, and liberal arts. Something productive, worthy, and with lasting influence."

James shakes his head and smiles. "And I guess it'll be called Fink U?"

As I chuckle, so do many of those standing around us, as one says, "That's a noble gesture, Mr. Fink."

As more laughter ensues, I wave my hand. "No, no, it is not Fink, it's Finkelstein. And *no*, my college will be called Van Der Veen University."

The man squints. "From the Swamp?"

As we all chuckle, I reply, "Yes, sir. From the Swamp. That's where my spiritual awakening came from. Even a mentor can learn from his protégé." Turning toward James, I add, "I only wish you would have balled me out sooner."

James smiles and helps me up to my feet. "Well, Jay, it truly warms my heart to hear that. As they say, 'better late than never.'"

I nod thoughtfully. "And please forgive me for the insensitive digs I often hurled at you. In fact, I like the color pink, and just might buy a shirt like yours."

James chuckles. Then, with a warm embrace, my friend escorts me out of the museum, leaving the bizarre world of illusion behind, along with my once-rotten ways.

Many will revile and judge me, I'm sure, but my future is now in God's hands, whatever that may be.

THE HELICON

The deafening roar of cheers was well deserved, as the cast of *Jersey Boys* took their bows. Adding to the cacophony of applause were the clapping hands of Gabrielle LaPierre and the shrill of Ronald DeSanto's whistle, which was amplified by his two pinkies stuck in the corners of his mouth.

Exiting the theater, hand in hand, the young couple, each twenty-eight years old, was celebrating their third anniversary of dating. Having previously dined at *Carmine's* Italian restaurant on 44th Street, they then collected their ten-year old Honda Accord from the iPark garage and headed toward home, through the Lincoln Tunnel, and eventually arrived at their small apartment in Hoboken, New Jersey.

As Ronald danced up the stairs to their second-floor pad, his mind reeled with curiosity, eager to know what other songs the Four Seasons had written.

He plopped down in front of his laptop and turned it on, then reached over and picked up his Fender Stratocaster. While he strummed a few chords, waiting for their slow modem to connect, Gabrielle sat at the small dinette table and pulled out her pink iPad. As she hummed the tune of *Rag Doll*, she brushed the long blonde hair out of her eyes and was about to begin typing, when she said, "You know what, honey, we should try writing songs like them. Our retro stuff is getting stale. We need something new and fresh for our gigs."

"Agreed, sweetheart," Ronald replied as he finally logged onto Wikipedia.

Gabrielle sat motionless, her mind in a rut like an old stylus skipping on a Four Seasons' 45. "Jesus, I can't even think of a good topic to write lyrics on," she said, frustrated.

Ronald chuckled. "Give it time, Gabby. We just walked in the door, for Pete's sake." Just then, his eyes landed on a tantalizing title; it was an album listed on the Four Seasons' discography. "Hey! How about *Helicon*?"

Gabrielle squinted. "Helik—what?"

"*Helicon*," Ronald said. "H-e-l-i-c-o-n. It's the name of an album by the Four Seasons, and their title song."

"Hmm, sounds interesting," Gabrielle said as she jotted the word down. "But what the heck does it mean?"

"Don't know. That's *why* it's interesting." He surfed over to Amazon.com and clicked on the audio sample of the title song, which, after a few seconds, included the lyrics *"Take me to Helicon, I want to write my song."*

Gabrielle's head recoiled as she sprung up and quick-paced over to Ronald's side. Intrigued, she peered down at the computer screen. "Hmm, I thought Helicon was some sort of Silicon or Helium. You mean it's a place?"

Ronald glanced up at her. "Yeah, it sounds like it."

"So where the heck *is* Helicon?"

"I'm surfing right now, babe. Ah, here we are!"

Gabrielle's eyes widened. "It's a mountain?"

"Yessiree. And it's in Boeotia, Greece."

"Jesus, that's a far cry from the Four Seasons' songs of love or rejection." She rubbed her chin. "I wonder what brought their attention all the way over to Greece for inspiration?"

Ronald gazed up at her. "Don't know. But since our songs have been mighty dull lately, what do you say we take a trip to this mysterious Helicon Mountain?"

Gabrielle smiled. "Sounds good to me. Take me to Helicon, I want to write my song!"

The couple landed in Athens International Airport, rented a SUV, and drove for two hours before they finally approached Mount Helicon. They strapped on their hiking gear, locked the vehicle, and began their adventurous journey up the mountain. Along the trail they came upon other travelers, two of which spoke English. They each exchanged stories about their previous hiking expeditions and, before long, they had scaled three-quarters of the way up. But suddenly, in the distance, thunderclouds roared and the skies blackened. Fearful of lightning, the other travelers turned around and headed for their cars.

Ronald sighed as his eyes peered nervously around. "Shoot! I guess we should follow them."

Gabrielle shook her head. "We're too far up to turn back now. We'll get drenched either way. I say we look for cover. We have rain gear."

Ronald gazed up nervously at the ominous sky as thunder rumbled. "It's not only rain, Gabby. The higher we go, the closer we'll be to the heavens. And we are in Greece now, so...who knows? Zeus might get pissed and hurl thunderbolts at us!"

Gabrielle shook her head and chuckled. "You're a knucklehead, Ronnie. I guess that's why I love you."

As Ron smiled and pulled up his hood, she glanced around and added, "And if we veer off this beaten path, just over there to the right, I think we can probably find cover, away from this open terrain."

"I'm game, Gabby. Lead the way."

Together they hiked into unknown territory, speckled with trees and large boulders, when the malignant clouds finally released their venom. Heavy rain pummeled the mountainside, as a river of water and mud swept downward. Ron and Gabrielle each grabbed onto the trunks of sturdy trees, yet the turbulent deluge ripped the trees and their human cargo loose of their moorings and rumbled down the mountainside. As they cascaded over rocks and debris, holding on for dear life, Gabrielle's tree smashed into a boulder, and her body slid down several yards until she grabbed onto a surviving tree. Ron saw what happened and let go. With determination, he fought his way through the mudslide and eventually reached her side.

Gabrielle gazed into his eyes, trembling, as Ron said with a smile, "Excellent idea to say up here, sweetheart. What's a little rain. Right?"

Just then, a bolt of lightning struck a tree some twenty feet away, blowing it apart as flames and smoke billowed. Blasted from her tree, Gabrielle grunted as she fell to the ground, while Ron wheezed as he was punched backward by the powerful discharge.

Gabrielle quickly jumped to her feet and used her hand as a visor to scan the area. "Ron, look over there! It looks like a cave!"

Swiftly, they dashed through the torrential downpour and lightning and entered the musty cavern.

Ron bent over as he tried to catch his breath. "Great find, sweetheart. As long as a bear doesn't live here."

Nervously, Gabrielle spun around and pulled out her knife. "Don't worry, honey. I have a Bowie!"

Ron chuckled nervously. "Well, I don't think a Bowie will be of any help, sweetheart, be it a knife or David himself. One will get us both killed, and the other is already dead." He bowed his head. "Quite regrettably, on both accounts."

Gabrielle gazed down at her knife. "You really think it's useless? What about if you distract him while I attack him from behind?"

Again Ronald chuckled, yet this time his voice cracked. "Sweetheart, you'd need a l-lot of muscle to break the bear's skin with that knife." Nervously, he glanced around. "Let's just hope there isn't a bear here. Or if there is, that the Olympian gods send Hercules to rip its jaw apart."

Gabrielle giggled. "I really appreciate that you're the funniest when we're up shit's creek."

"Well, if we're gonna die, we might as well die laughing, right?"

"Okay, enough of the clowning around." She pointed the Bowie knife toward the dark abyss of the cave. "Let's see what the hell is really in here."

"Fine," Ron said as he whipped the rain out of his wavy black hair. "But since you have the knife, I guess that means you'll lead."

Gabrielle twisted her lips. "Very well. But Hercules you're not!"

"Sure. Make your digs. But for your information, I'm more valuable than Hercules." He switched on his Rayovac flashlight. "I'm Apollo, the Sun God!"

"Well, a sunny disposition is all you have, honey."

With that, Gabrielle proceeded to walk into the blackened tunnel as 'Apollo' cautiously lit her way from behind. To their surprise, the tunnel was much longer and more winding than they anticipated, yet fortunately it harbored no bears, just rocks and moss, as trickles of rainwater cascaded down the craggy walls. Moments later, they came upon something that froze Gabrielle in her tracks. She gasped for air and peered back at Ron. "Jesus! It's a dead body. And holy cow, does it stink!"

Ron covered his nose as he stepped ahead of her and knelt down by the half-rotted corpse. The man's face was a putrid display of scant muscle tissue dangling loosely from his skull, while his clothes remained partially intact, save for the shredded holes on the man's bloody sleeves, revealing huge claw and bite marks. Meanwhile, one leg had been completely severed off and sat three feet away.

"Oh, shit!" Ron exclaimed, his voice riddled with fear. "This man and his parts are stored goods. We gotta get outta here! Fast!"

Spinning around, Ron froze. Crawling up behind Gabrielle was the bear; mid-sized, but not happy.

"Behind you!" he screamed, as he veered left and waved the flashlight in the bear's eyes. Irritated, the young beast blinked. Gabrielle followed Ron's lead and crouched down as the bear wobbled semi-blind past her. When it did, she lunged up from behind and dragged the Bowie across the bear's throat. The beast let out a fierce roar, laced with agony, as it attempted to swing around toward its assailant. But while Gabrielle latched onto its back, jabbing at its jugular, Ron ran headfirst into the bear's stomach, which knocked the wind out of him. Then, with a right upper cut, Ron rammed the butt-end of the metal Rayovac into the bear's genitals.

The light in the cave flickered and the furry beast wailed, as the fight for survival continued. Gabrielle continued choking the animal's slit throat, while Ron issued blows to the bear's stomach and groin. The frenzy lasted only ten more seconds, until the bear gagged on his own blood and fell dead. Yet, to the heroic couple, the skirmish felt like fifty minutes of pure terror.

Sitting exhausted on the cave floor next to their bloody kill, the two 28-year olds from Hoboken sighed, then almost cried, as their bodies trembled with tingling waves of adrenaline. Meanwhile, sweat poured down their pale faces, as the flashlight miraculously continued to shine, flickering at random intervals.

Having regained her composure, Gabrielle gazed at Ron and smiled. "You see, like I said, all you had to do was distract it while I sliced its jugular."

Ron finally managed to chuckle his fear away. "I guess so. And by the way, you were magnificent!"

"So were you, Apollo. You have courage after all." She wiped her bloody Bowie and arms clean on the bear's fur, then slipped the knife back in its sleeve. She looked down at the bear. "And who knows, maybe this hairy beast will make it into one of our songs."

"Yeah, I suppose we can sing how our nightmare in Hades was un*bear*able!"

Gabrielle smiled as she stood up and glanced around. That's when her eyes spotted something in the shadows, and she pointed. "Hey! Shine the light over there!"

Ron shook the flickering flashlight, which snapped steadily on, and pointed it in the direction she indicated. There, caught in the Rayovac's narrow beam, was a shapely clay storage jar, decorated with classical Greek etchings. "Wow!" Ron exclaimed. "Could that be what I think it is?"

"Do you think it's real? I mean, an actual relic from ancient Greece?"

"Good god, Gabby, it certainly looks like it."

As Gabrielle approached it, she realized it had a cover on it, which, to her surprise, was locked. She picked it up and held the decorative jar in the beam of the flashlight. "Look at this. It appears to have a combination-type lock built into it with Greek letters."

Ron squinted. "I don't recall ever reading or hearing about ancient jars having combination locks. So it's probably a cheap modern replica." Eyeing it up closely, he mimicked a British actor in a Greek play, as he declared, "When we get out of Hades alive, Aphrodite my dear, we should have an oracle in Athens examine it. Of course, that's if we don't run into a bloody Minotaur on our way out."

With smiles and giggles, the couple waited for the storm to pass, then eagerly descended Mount Helicon.

Upon arriving back in Athens, they brought the clay jar to *Damocles's Antiquities* to be appraised. The shop owner deferred to his specialist, who gave the final verdict: The *pithos*, or storage jar, was dated to be from approximately 670 to 700 BC, and valued at anywhere from $35,000 to $65,000—even more if they could open it. He explained that the combination lock was a baffling oddity, never having heard of one in that era, especially on a *pithos*. And since it was sophisticated enough not to be opened with simple entries, it made his appraisal much lower than it would likely receive in an auction at *Sotheby's* or *Christie's*. Elated with their rare find, the young couple caught the next plane home.

Eleven hours later, they landed at Newark Airport. On their way home, Ron glanced at the carefully packaged box that contained their prized *pithos*. "I'm really not thrilled about bringing this to our apartment, Gabby. How about we stop at the Liberty Science Center? I'm sure they can store it safely and properly. And perhaps there's someone there who might know something more about it."

With a nod from Gabrielle, Ron veered off the New Jersey Turnpike and entered the parking lot of the Science Center. Gabrielle carried the precious package into the facility, placed it on the counter, and explained her find. As the *pithos* emerged from the bubble wrap, the staff crowded around. Four sets of eyes widened as the heads of four scientists almost collided in their zeal to get a closer look.

Paul Danbury, the manager, was intrigued by the rare find as he ran his fingers across its unique cover, then gazed up at Gabrielle. "I've never seen an artifact this old with a combination lock. Do you happen to know the code?"

"I'm afraid not. Do you know of anyone who might have an idea?"

"Not offhand, as there's never been a case like this, to my knowledge." He peered back down at the combination tumblers. "And since these seven tumblers have Greek letters, I imagine it will be a little more difficult to decode." He looked back up at Gabrielle. "Feel free to sit in my office while I track down Professor Justin Herald. He's our maven of antiquities."

With that, Danbury left, as Gabrielle and Ron brought the *pithos* into Danbury's office. Ron sat in Danbury's chair and immediately pulled out his cell phone and clicked open his browser.

Gabrielle crossed her arms, mimicking his mother. "Ronnie! Get out of his seat! And what are you doing?"

"I'm searching *Mount Helicon and Greece in 700 BC.*"

Gabrielle rolled her eyes. "Do you really think you'll find the person who knew the combination to a rare jar lost in a bear cave in 700 BC?" Condescendingly, she snickered. "Get real, Sherlock!"

"Hey, every specialist agreed: this is a rare, one-of-a-kind find. So, we can sit here and wait for another specialist—who, let's face it, won't know much more than we do about how to open it—or we can try to solve this mystery ourselves."

Ron thumbed through several web pages and came upon several related items; one made him smile. "Look here! My search on Mount Helicon mentions the Four Seasons. How about that?"

Gabrielle smirked. "Oh, *Ronnie, Ronnie, Ronnie, I'll never know*…what to do with you!"

Ron glanced up. "Okay. Never mind the Four Seasons shtick, but this is the season to be jolly, because I think I figured out the combo."

"Very funny."

"No, I'm serious. In fact, dead serious, emphasis on *dead*."

Now intrigued, Gabrielle strode over and peered down at his cell phone. She grasped his hand and pulled the phone closer. "What the heck do you mean by *dead*? And how can you possibly know the combination? Did Lord Google, the omniscient wizard, have the answer?"

"No, Google had nothing to do with it. And no one posted the combo, sweetie. I figured it out. Plain and simple deduction, just like *Sherlock*. Of course, I could be wrong, but I'm more disturbed by the premise of this rare *pithos* than anything else. You see, I learned that a very famous Greek author lived in 700 BC, the time our lovely jar was made, and he happened to live in—of all places— Boeotia."

Gabrielle smiled as she kissed him on the forehead and sat on his lap. "Okay, this *is* getting interesting. But I hope there's more to it than that. I mean, what makes you think that it had to be a famous author who's connected to this jar? Why couldn't it be some regular Joe Blow?"

"Because this famous Greek author, who lived near Mount Helicon, wrote a very famous tale, one that is quite frightening. And that's why I can't tell you the combination."

Gabrielle stood up, annoyed. "Are you kidding me? You can't tease me like that, and then not tell me. That's mean, cruel, and just not like you."

Ron swiveled in Danbury's chair, then stood up. "Listen, Gabby. I know how eager you are to open this *pithos*. So was I, until I read what this very well might be."

"Well, if you don't tell me, I'll just go online and find out myself."

He tossed the phone on Danbury's desk, and crossed his arms. "Fine, go ahead. But I'm not going to be a party to this."

Gabrielle dashed to the phone and read through the pages, as Ron looked at the jar with trepidation. Picking it up, he rotated it slowly to look at its finely etched designs and at the ominous cover with its unique combination lock, securing the scary contents within. Gingerly, he put it down and glanced over at Gabrielle, who finally looked up, clearly deep in thought.

Ron walked over to her, and pleaded, "Gabby, please! Leave this jar be. In fact, we should bury it someplace where no one will ever find it."

A devious smile grew on Gabrielle's face as she nodded slowly. "I believe I figured it out, Mr. Holmes. The Greek author was Hesiod, and what I've also learned is that one of his famous tales included a *pithos*. However, the article says that many centuries later, Erasmus rewrote the tale in English, and translated the word *pithos* as 'box.'"

Ron's head fell, knowing it was only a matter of time before she figured it out, and time was running out quickly, time that would soon unleash unthinkable woes for mankind, as Gabrielle declared, "That tale was called *Pandora's Box*!"

Ron raised his hand in caution. "Gabby! Listen to what you're saying. You *cannot* open this box!"

Gabrielle stood up and strode over to the *pithos*. "And do you hear yourself, Ronnie? Do you mean to say you're scared of a Greek myth? Are you also afraid of the Minotaur or the Cyclops? Come on!" She picked up the antique jar and flicked the tumblers with her finger, as her eyes gazed at the odd Greek letters. "So, I guess Pandora's Box must open with her name. Seven letters, seven tumblers."

"Gabby, stop! Don't do this. I'm serious!"

"No, sweetie, you're delirious. You're acting like a child. It wasn't Zeus who threw those thunderbolts at us on Mount Helicon, was it?" Ron shook his head, annoyed, as she went on, "And it wasn't a Minotaur that we killed in the cave, was it?"

"I don't find you funny, Gabby!"

"And I don't find you sane, Ronnie. I truly can't believe how you're behaving over this silly myth." She gazed back down at the box, and flipped the tumblers to spell PANDORA with the aid of a Greek alphabet chart on Ron's cell phone. As she flipped the tumblers, Ron looked on, relaxed, as she finally reached the last letter. She twisted the cover, but to no avail. Perplexed, she looked up at Ron, who smiled. "So, Ronnie boy, you think it's funny?"

Ron crossed his arms, leaned back against the wall, and raised his eyebrows with a sly smirk.

"No biggie," she retorted. "Eventually I'll get it." Her eyes oscillated as her mind searched for the connection. Suddenly, she stopped. "I've got it! It's Helicon!" Eagerly, she turned the tumblers and twisted hard, but only her hand turned, as the cover remained fixed. She gritted her teeth, then entered one guess after another, but only achieved a string of failures, as her frustration grew with each failed attempt.

Livid, she placed the box down, harder than she should have, which alarmed Ron, as he yelled, "Jesus! Be careful, Gabby!"

"Enough of playing Jeopardy. What is it?" she barked.

"So you want the question?"

"Don't be cute, Ron. I'm not in the mood. You know I never could play Jeopardy anyhow, so give me the answer in question form, if that'll make you happy."

"Not opening Pandora's Box is what will make me happy, Gabby."

Just then, Paul Danbury walked in with Professor Herald, who immediately strode over to the unique jar. He picked it up and marveled at the exquisite detail and its highly abnormal combination lock. "This is a magnificent find. I'm told you found it in a cave on Mount Helicon, is that correct?"

"Yes, Professor Herald," Gabrielle said excitedly as she stepped alongside him. "We also believe this might very well be the famous, or perhaps infamous, Pandora's Box."

The professor looked at her as he continued to hold the prized artifact. "And you might very well be correct." He glanced back down at the tumblers, and added, "Did you happen to figure out the combination?"

Gabrielle looked at Ron. "Well, *I* didn't, but my boyfriend says he has."

Professor Herald removed his glasses and placed the coveted box down. "If that's so, why haven't you opened it yet?"

Irritably, Ron uncrossed his arms and pushed himself away from the wall. "You're a professor of ancient history and you're asking *me* why we didn't open Pandora's Box? Are you kidding me!"

The professor smiled. "Mr. DeSanto, I see that you are young, but you certainly weren't born yesterday. Do you seriously believe a worldwide calamity will spring out of this little clay jar? A promise that was fabricated from the fanciful mind of an ancient Greek poet?"

"At your age you should know that there is just as much fiction in facts as there are facts in fiction."

"*Touché*, Mr. DeSanto. But honestly, who nowadays even believes in the Olympian gods? No one. Correction, there may be a handful of quacks out there who do, but really, are you going to contend that they are rational?"

"Well, you should know that for thousands of years the majority of the world believed the Earth was flat. Yet a few *quacks* turned an entire globe's worth of highbrowed fools on their heads."

The professor smirked and fumbled with his glasses as Ron added, "I'm not saying I believe in the vast majority of Greek mythology, Professor, but could there be an ounce of truth hidden somewhere within those tales? And God forbid this tale is the one that happens to be true."

The professor just shrugged Ron's rhetoric aside as he replied, "Listen, son, I cannot force you to open the box. But I guarantee you that once you sell it to a museum; they will most assuredly open it. Moreover, there might be something of great value inside that will augment your girlfriend's selling price. So, why waste time?"

"He's right," Gabrielle finally said, exasperated. "I want it opened before I sell it. So, please, tell me the combo."

Ron's head dropped. "I'm sorry, Gabby. But I just can't."

Meanwhile, the professor had been calculating in his head as he slipped his glasses in his pocket. Then, as if he had won Lotto, his eyes widened. "Yes, of course. I've got it!"

Gabrielle's face lit up, while fear rattled Ron.

With a smug grin the professor looked at Gabrielle. "You said you entered Pandora, Helicon, and other words with seven digits, yet you never entered the most important one—the name of the author."

Gabrielle squinted. "But Hesiod is only six letters."

"Yes, in English, but in Greek it is spelled Ἡ-σ-ί-ο-δ-ο-ς. Seven letters."

Gabrielle looked at Ron, who glanced at the wall and closed his eyes. Eagerly, she grasped the box and turned the tumblers. Reaching the last letter, she twisted…

And still, nothing happened.

Her smile of anticipation withered to a frown of frustration. She gazed at the professor and moaned, "That's not it, either."

Ron opened his eyes, elated that the expert was also wrong, when the box slipped from Gabrielle's hands. As it slid down, she grabbed the cover's handle, which pulled up and partially unlocked the *pithos*! Gabrielle's face illuminated with a grin. With a slight twist, Gabrielle fully opened Pandora's Box!

Ron cringed, as Gabrielle, Herald, and Danbury each rushed to gaze inside the *pithos*. Their three faces, glowing with expectation, mellowed to portraits of disappointment. Gabrielle placed the jar down, reached in, and pulled out the only item inside: a peculiar, dried-out plant.

Baffled, she inquired, "What is this?"

Professor Herald and Danbury gazed at the lackluster find, as Herald responded, "Evidently, it's some type of foreign plant. I'm not a botanist, so…" Turning toward Danbury, he said, "Perhaps we should call in Jacqueline Harvey?"

"Indeed," Danbury replied.

Moments later, Botanist Jacqueline Harvey entered the room and inspected the specimen. She looked at Gabrielle. "Very, very odd. This species, Miss LaPierre, does not exist, at least not in our present era. However, it is a type of *Dionaea muscipula*."

"A Diona…what?"

"A *Dionaea muscipula*. A species akin to a Venus flytrap."

Ron sprang forward. "A Venus flytrap? A *carnivore*?"

Jacqueline laughed. "Have no fear, Mr. DeSanto. Carnivorous plants cannot eat anything larger than insects, and on very rare occasions, perhaps a very small frog."

While all the others in the room giggled, Ron twisted his lips as he gazed at the withered plant. "Well, this carnivore looks dead anyhow, and it sure as hell ought to be. It's almost three thousand years old, right?"

"Well, age is not always a factor," Jacqueline replied. "On very rare occasions I'm able to rejuvenate old plants. And for its age, this specimen is very well preserved. In fact, exceptionally well preserved."

"Oh, swell!" Ron huffed, to another round of condescending giggles. He looked at the lot of them with incredulous eyes. "So, you mean to say that you truly believe that someone three thousand years ago placed this weird, carnivorous plant in a jar, and sealed it shut with a sophisticated locking mechanism, just on a whim? Why? Just for the fun of it?"

As they each paused to reflect on his meaningful words, Jacqueline responded, "Well, I don't know about all the historical abnormalities associated with this artifact, but the plant's preservation may have been due to the fact that the jar seems to have been airtight. As such, the lack of exposure to oxygen substantially slowed down the decaying process. In modern terms, it was vacuum sealed."

Ron smacked the desk and snickered. "There you go! So we have another *extremely unique* aspect to this *extremely weird* jar and its *extremely frightening* contents. And yet you're all being *extremely complacent*?"

Danbury nodded. "Yes, this artifact has some very unique properties, Ronald, but we are scientists, and as such, we are not being complacent. On the contrary, we revel when we're confronted with rarities like this."

He picked up the jar and inspected it briefly once again, then gazed over at Gabrielle. "So I take it this artifact belongs to you?" As Gabrielle nodded, he added, "Well, we have special labs and greenhouses here where we can not only secure it for you but also make sure it's well maintained, with regulated temperature and proper humidity levels. Of course, that's if you wish for us to secure it and study it while you seek avenues of procuring a buyer?"

Gabrielle peered at Ron. "Well, what do you say? It was your idea to have them store it here safely."

Ron shrugged. "It's your box, Pandora, and you already opened it. So do what you want."

Gabrielle smirked, then turned toward Danbury and acknowledged her approval. She received a contract detailing the facility's responsibilities, while also indicating that ownership of the artifact belonged to Gabrielle LaPierre. With the signing of the document and the careful storage of the artifact, the couple drove home in their old Honda. The ride was as much a vacuum of silence as the *pithos* had been for three millennia.

As they entered their small apartment, they both realized there was no place to hide. Uneasily, they looked at each other, waiting to see who would break the silence. Ron took the lead. "So, now that you've unleashed a carnivorous monster into the world, I'm just *dying* for a nice, meaty steak."

Gabrielle wasn't sure if he was being sarcastic or jesting, and just stood there, uncomfortable and mute, until Ron smiled and said, "Come on, you crazy, reckless woman, let's make something to eat."

With an embrace and pecks on each of their cheeks, the couple grilled up two steaks and vegetables and enjoyed a candlelit dinner; she drank Chianti, he a Budweiser.

Afterward, they retired to the couch. Ron picked up his guitar and plucked out a few new riffs, while Gabrielle sat with her iPad, wrestling with lyrics. After several hours, they crafted five new songs, each containing lyrics pertaining to their eventful journey and miraculous find.

"These new songs are quite good, honey," Gabrielle said. "They're exactly what we ventured to Greece for."

Ron nodded as he plucked a few strings with his ear close to the fret board. "Yes, indeed they are. Let's hope that with the money you make on that *pithos* we can produce and market this new album once its finished." As he twisted a tuning peg, he sheepishly looked at her. "Perhaps you were right. Maybe that jar was a gift—our ticket to finally breaking into the major music industry."

Gabrielle didn't wish to gloat, but was happy he'd finally abandoned his childish fear. "Well, for the past four years we sure as heck have struggled to build a following. So yes, this feels good, Ron. Like it was our destiny."

As they resumed rehearsing their new songs, their session was abruptly halted when their neighbor banged on the shared wall, and yelled, "Ron, I love your guitar work, really, and Gabrielle, your voice is lovely, but it's eleven o'clock. So please, *shut the hell up!*"

With chuckles, the two disbanded and retired for the night.

The following week went by faster than either realized, as Gabrielle got back into the grind at work, being a receptionist at a local healthcare facility, while Ron waited on tables at a local Italian restaurant. But beyond those conventional day jobs, their true dream was to be the next Sonny and Cher or Ike and Tina Turner, minus the divorce or abuse. Their retro-flavored gigs on weekends or at functions had been a tough grind, but they were making minor waves and hoped to continue on their ultimate quest.

Eager to test out their five new songs, Ron looked forward to the evening's gig at a local bar in Hoboken. But as always, life had a way of derailing noble pursuits, as the phone rang.

Jacqueline Harvey was on the other end, elated. The botanist managed to not only get the extinct plant to root and grow, but had other exciting news, as well, as she added, "You see, Gabrielle, the *Dionaea muscipula* has a healthy reproduction system. Their roots develop bulbs, which in turn create whole new plants. And your lovely new species has already produced eight other plants!"

Gabrielle was ecstatic. "My God, that's incredible. Is that normal?"

"Well, the *Dionaea muscipula* species are asexual and do reproduce in this manner, but never at this accelerated rate. You must come and see this, because they have also grown far larger than any of its sibling species currently in existence."

Gabrielle turned and looked at Ron on the couch, about to relay the amazing news, but paused. She turned her back to him and walked furtively toward the apartment door, as she whispered, "I'll run right over," and quickly hung up.

She slipped on a sweater. "I'll be back in an hour or two, honey."

But as her hand grasped the doorknob, he called out, "Wait a minute!" as he stood up. "We have our gig tonight at *Finnegan's Pub*. We need to set up in less than an hour."

"Okay, so I'll make it quick, and be back in thirty minutes."

"Yeah right! *You* do something quick? Never happened. I just heard you say an hour or two. Now you say a half hour? No way." Grabbing his guitar, he added, "We've been practicing these new songs all week, and I'm dying to test them out. Come on, you even agreed, this would take precedence over that crazy jar."

"How did you know it was—"

"Listen, anything that makes you forget about our music has to be something major, or money-related. And what's even worse is that you tried hiding it from me."

"Fine, so why don't you come with me then? This way, you can drag my tush out of there when you're ready to leave."

"Invitation accepted!"

With that, the couple drove to the Liberty Science Center and met Jacqueline Harvey, who escorted them to her special horticultural greenhouse. Ron and Gabrielle's eyes widened at the sight before them. The inordinate sizes of the plants are what first startled them, being that they grew to be two feet tall in one week, not to mention that there were now nine plants with eighty-one healthy sprouts breaking ground.

Ron was thunderstruck as he clutched his chest. "Dear God! This is incredible!" As Jacqueline and Gabrielle smiled, he added, "I mean, incredibly scary."

Jacqueline walked over to the robust plant and patted it gently, like a pet. "Ron, these plants are not scary. They're an amazing, ancient species that we've been fortunate enough to revive. It's truly a miracle."

"A miracle, or an ill omen?" he replied, his fears now also revived. "Just how fast will they grow, and how big will they get?"

"There is no way of knowing, Ron. As I said, this species is an anomaly. That's why I'm all the more eager to monitor and record their progression as they reach full maturity."

Gabrielle crouched down to get a closer look at the plant. "I agree, these plants are amazing." She rose back up and held her chin as she looked over all nine plants, as if their proud mother, and said, "I think this species needs a name. I'll call it Helicon." She turned back toward Ron. "Just like the mountain we found it on. Do you agree?"

Ron nodded mechanically. "Sure, why not? So long as this Helicon monster doesn't give us a mountain of problems."

Jacqueline shook her head with a reassuring smile. "Don't worry, Ron, as I said, there has never been a man-eating plant. And these wondrous Helicons are a delightful addition to our ecosystem."

Opening a plastic container filled with ants, she grasped one and placed it on one of the Helicon's clam-shaped leaves with its large, needlelike teeth. In a split second, the spiked leaf clamped down tight on the ant, rendering it dead in seconds as the plant's toxic juices began its digestive process. Jacqueline explained how Venus flytraps generally take five to twelve days to digest an insect, then open up to expel the exoskeleton. However, the Helicon digests its prey in four hours, exoskeleton included. Although Gabrielle found this to be fascinating, the same couldn't be said for Ron, who fretfully grasped her arm and escorted her out of the building to their car. As Gabrielle admonished him about the rude exit, Ron didn't say a word as he headed for *Finnegan's Pub*.

Two weeks passed when Gabrielle received another phone call. This time, Jacqueline had even better news to convey. The Helicons had multiplied so rapidly that they cleared out another greenhouse to make room for her unique and prolific plant. What's more, they had grown to be six feet tall, an unheard of size for the species. Its spiked clamshell leaves were now the size of a football, and had also introduced a new anomaly—they'd eaten several rats, and a squirrel. As Gabrielle nearly choked, Jacqueline said she hadn't even relayed the grandest bit of news.

Jacqueline had invited other scientists to analyze various properties of the plant. One of them, namely Dr. Kildare from ExxonMobil Corp., discovered that the Helicon plant produced a unique enzyme. And when mixed with processed corn oil, the enzyme produced a clean energy source that had none of the toxic side effects of fossil fuel, and was ten times more efficient.

Despite Ron's fears of the plant's aberrant growth and deadly appetite, he was elated about the new enzyme that would eliminate the disastrous effects of fossil fuel and enhance the gas mileage of cars tenfold. Meanwhile, Gabrielle wasted no time taking advantage of the financial windfall that soon fell upon her like an avalanche, as she received advances from all the major oil companies to buy large quantities of the new enzyme to produce—what Gabrielle called—Helicon-X fuel. With the millions of dollars that rolled in, Gabrielle established *Helicon-E*, her own corporation, and set up massive greenhouses in ten locations throughout the country to mass-produce the enzyme. Within two years, Helicon-X fuel had become the miracle of the age, as Gabrielle's millions turned into billions.

Having moved into a penthouse in Jersey City, the couple was now in their new standard positions: her at the computer, where she managed her enormous corporation, while he sat on the couch and strummed his Stratocaster.

As she busily plugged numbers into her Excel spreadsheet, Gabrielle glanced up at Ron and huffed, "Can you please do that somewhere else? I'm trying to concentrate on important matters."

"Oh, so once again, *music* doesn't matter, right? I thought our shared dream was to focus on a musical career. You haven't had time to join me at any of the gigs I've had over the last two years, let alone compose anything new."

Gabrielle rolled her eyes as she tried to maintain her focus. "Are you serious? How can you compare the billions

I'm making to earning pocket change with music? That's *billions*, darling, with a 'B!'"

Ron smirked, as he turned his head and muttered, "And you've become an s.o.b, with a 'B!'"

"What was that?"

Ron shook his head. "Never mind. I was actually going to ask you something else, something very important, but I guess even that would take up too much of your precious time." He reached over and put his guitar back in its rack, then stared vacantly at the wall.

Meanwhile, Gabrielle returned to plugging in her ten-digit numbers, when suddenly she stopped. She peered over at Ron, who sat dejectedly on the couch. She huffed, then said, "Okay. What is it?"

Ron looked over. "I put it in your desk, since that's where you grew roots, like your precious Helicon."

Gabrielle ignored the insult and squinted. "Right here, in my desk?"

"Yes. I put it there two hours ago, when you actually left your seat to take a leak. I think you *might* like it."

She pushed herself away from the desk and opened the drawer. Inside was a blue velvet box. She picked it up and looked at him. "For me?"

Ron stood up and walked over. He grasped the box, opened it, and knelt on one knee. "Gabrielle, will you be my wife?"

Gabrielle was totally caught off guard. Granted, she knew they had been dating for five years, and the time was ripe. But she had been so consumed with *Helicon-E* and the billions that were rolling in, she'd not only neglected finding time to sell the priceless *pithos*, but had neglected Ron, almost completely.

Ron gazed deep into her blue eyes as he took the one-carat diamond ring out of the blue box. He extended it toward her and said, "I know it's a trifle, sweetheart, but on my meager salary, that's all I can afford."

Gabrielle smirked. "I told you many times you could use the account I set up for you. It has a million dollars in it. Yet I see my money isn't good enough for you. You haven't even withdrawn a single cent."

"I don't want your money, Gabby. I want *you*! Always have."

"That's very touching, honey. But our marriage will require a prenuptial agreement just the same."

He stood up, tossed the ring on her desk, and vented, "There you go again! Everything revolves around money with you. I've told you a billion times: I have *no* interest in your billions! You may have opened Pandora's Box for riches, but I opened this little blue box to give you my heart and soul, my unconditional love for all eternity."

Gabrielle tried to backpedal. "Okay, I'm sorry. What more do you want from me?"

"I want your love and attention, that's what. But I've received neither over the past two years. Perhaps that is the curse of opening Pandora's Box!"

She twisted her lips, as if a chunk of Limburger cheese was in her mouth, rolled her eyes, then turned back to her Excel sheet.

"So *that's* your frigid response to my warm declaration of love?"

She gazed up at him, while still typing, and said, "You consider *that* warm? Constantly badgering me and putting a tacky blue box, with a tiny diamond ring, in my desk drawer?"

"Good God! I can't stand your haughty bullshit anymore! Or your avaricious obsession."

"And you're a naïve, daydreaming wannabe," Gabrielle sneered. "I've made more money than I ever dreamed of, and I showered you with a new car, new clothes, this penthouse, and all the most expensive foods and wines on this planet. Yet, you still want to be a silly rock star. Grow up!"

Ron gritted his teeth, then fired back, "I never wanted millions or billions or all of your fancy, highfalutin gifts. They mean nothing without being able to share them with someone you love. And let's face it, our love evaporated the day you opened that damn box! It sucked the oxygen right out of my lungs and dreams, dreams that I thought we both shared. But I was wrong. Your dream was just to get rich. My dream was to give something from my heart to the world that would transcend time."

Gabrielle clapped tepidly. "Bravo! That was a wonderful, heartfelt performance. But in case you haven't noticed, Helicon-X is a miraculous discovery that has enhanced the entire world. Most oil companies have been using my enzyme to make the most fuel-efficient product to ever grace this polluted planet. It's one hundred-percent pure, gloriously green. So you want to talk about transcending time? No piece of music could ever have the global and life-saving effect as Helicon-X!"

Ron shook his head. "And if that Helicon plant in that jar was dead and incapable of being revived, your billions and transcending discovery would have also been dead!"

"Whatever, Ron. But the fact is, it *did* yield a new enzyme, and it *did* enhance the world. So much for your whining and your infantile Pandora's Box phobia. Success is here, right under your nose. But if you can't see it and embrace it, then perhaps you should grab your dreamy little guitar and leave."

Ron gazed deeply into her cold blue eyes for an oddly long moment, unable to even speak the rest of his mind, then turned, picked up his Stratocaster, and walked toward the door. Before reaching it, he turned around and asked, "There's only one thing I'd like, if it's not too much trouble."

Gabrielle gazed at him with a deadpan stare, then nodded slightly, as Ron said, "I'd like the *pithos*."

She snorted as she rested her elbow on her desk and rubbed her full lips. "Hmm. A very valuable item. I thought money wasn't a priority?"

"It isn't. It's not the value I seek. It's the memory, a reminder of the box we actually found together that you opened, against my wishes, and destroyed our relationship for."

"Sure, it's yours." She whipped her long, blonde hair away from her pretty face and added, "You always were too sentimental. It's a vice you should seriously look to lose."

"Well, if it's anything like *you*, then you're right."

With that, Ron exited.

Gabrielle stared aimlessly at the ground for about three seconds, when she turned around and noticed the one-carat diamond ring on her desk. "Shit," she muttered as she grasped it, looked at the tiny stone, then threw it into the bottom drawer of her desk and kicked it shut. She got up and walked over to her custom wine closet, which she had built for thirty thousand dollars, and swung open the door. She scanned the sizable rack of various wines from all the best wineries across the globe, when her eyes landed on a winner. She took the coveted bottle, got herself a Riedel wine glass, and uncorked the bottle of Chateau Lafite 1787, worth $156,450.00, an extremely rare vintage from the cellar of Thomas Jefferson.

She took a sip and savored the rich, aged flavor. Then, upon reflection of what had just transpired, she thought, *You went on and on about your declaration of love, Ron, but here I am drinking a wine from the author of the Declaration of Independence. And damn, it tastes and feels great!!*

48

Sixteen months later, Gabrielle's stock prices were reaching an all-time high, yet lobbyists in Washington were leveling charges that she'd cornered the market and held a monopoly. Gabrielle invested millions in her own lobbyists and on broad media campaigns, which not only championed her entrepreneurial spirit and success as America's wealthiest self-made woman—which resonated with the public—but she emphasized the fact that it was her Helicon plant that produced the enzyme. And just like any inventor who offers something wholly unique to the world, they're entitled to its sole profits for a period of time until the patent expires. And hers had not yet reached its expiration date.

Having won the anti-trust legal battle, Gabrielle was celebrating in her penthouse with executives from her company and CEOs from her clients' companies. As waiters served hors d'oeuvres and bartenders mixed drinks and poured thousands of dollars of liquor per minute, Gabrielle made it a point to cajole her guests into maintaining their loyalty to her.

However, one guest at the party happened to be a rival's mole, who turned up the volume on the flat screen TV, having switched it from a golf tournament to the evening news. Aware of the report about to be announced, he nudged several guests to look at the screen, as the commentator reported:

"It has now been confirmed. The mysterious rise of deaths around the world due to the extreme increase in a new breed of army ant has finally been identified. And the prospect is bleak, as this has become a global epidemic."

As all the guests gazed at the screen with rapt attention, the commentator issued the deathblow:

"Scientists have discovered that the cause of this deadly phenomenon comes from Helicon-X fuel. Emissions of automobiles across the globe and from home heating systems have saturated the atmosphere, which is causing red army ants to mutate, whereby increasing their size and numbers, turning them into flying, killer ants."

As Gabrielle attempted to grab the remote, a guest from Shell Oil stayed her hand. "Leave it alone!" he demanded, as others echoed the reprimand.

Meanwhile the news broadcast continued to alarm all in attendance:

"The first signs of this deadly epidemic occurred over two years ago when the mauled remains of thousands of small animals across the globe were found. The cause was due to a new breed of army ant that somehow emerged, one that is the size of a locust, can fly like a locust, but like their *Eciton burchellii* species, are carnivorous and extremely deadly. Swarming in large numbers, these super killer ants not only turned to devouring large pigs and cattle at livestock ranches but have now mauled and devoured hundreds of thousands of humans worldwide as they fly into urban areas. Even their bite is toxic, as those lucky enough to have escaped their deadly jaws have remained paralyzed for weeks while many others have died. And the specific agent that's causing the ants' abnormal mutation and rapid reproduction is the emission of the Helicon enzyme found in the Helicon plant and in Helicon-X fuel. Worse still, scientists have no idea how to reverse this global epidemic."

While some guests dropped their wine glasses and ran toward the door, others frantically pulled out their cell phones and called either their loved ones (to see if they were safe) or their company's chemists (to instruct them to seek a solution). All, however, called their brokers to immediately sell their stocks of *Helicon-E.*

Gabrielle felt faint as she sat on the sofa with her ten thousand-dollar glass of wine. She took a sip, half dazed. Suddenly, it didn't taste so good anymore. In fact, it tasted downright flat.

In haste, guests fled out the door as if the building were on fire. Even Gabrielle's once loyal servants abandoned their employer. Soon she was left alone, just herself and her bottle of President Jefferson's wine by her side. Solemnly, she gazed at the bottle beside her, then noticed a coin in the seam of the seat cushion. She reached in with her fingers and pulled it out. It was a nickel. She gazed at Jefferson's cheap nickel-plated face, and snorted at the coincidence, then tossed it and Jefferson's bottle of wine into the fireplace. Her head fell as tears streamed down her forlorn face.

Meanwhile, Ron had likewise seen the news, and was devastated. He still carried a torch for his one and only love, and his heart burned with empathy for her catastrophic folly. Yet, he couldn't bring himself to see her. The wound was too deep, and he truly believed she had written him off, just like a tax credit, a mere trivial task amid the far more important grind of earning billions.

Perched beside Ron as he watched the news was his old buddy, Billy Shaffer. The great thing about old childhood friends is that they're always there for you during the ups and downs. But the downside is that they usually say exactly what's on their minds, without a filter.

Billy got up to fetch another beer, and offered his opinion. "Hey, look at the bright side, bro—you may have been grieving for the past year and a half, but that old broad of yours really screwed the entire world." He cracked open a bottle of Corona, and added, "She just had to open Pandora's Box, right? I mean, how stupid can that rich bitch be? They should string her up by her ovar—"

"Enough, Billy!" Ron snapped. "I know, I know. Remember? I lived with her, I love her, I get it."

Billy just had to get another jab in. "Ahh! Did you hear yourself? You said 'love her.' Present tense. You gotta let her go, bro. You're just as stupid for loving a deadly Black Widow as she is for opening that deadly box."

Ron stood up. "Enough already! Christ! I don't need your advice, Dr. Phil." Yet Ron couldn't get Billy's constant refrain out of his head, as he conceded, "But you're right about one thing, Billy boy."

Billy took a swig of Corona, and asked, "Yeah, and what's that? That you're stupid?"

Ron had to laugh. "Yes, I am, because I remained friends with *you!*"

Billy smiled as he plopped on the couch. "Okay, enough of this bullshit. Do you think someone can reverse this situation, before we all get eaten alive?"

"Well, that's the one good thing I was referring to, Billy. So I thank you for reminding me about how this all started. And that was back in Greece, with the bizarre myth that proved to be true. So, I need to read up on it again to see if there's something I missed."

Ron got up and walked over to his desk. He took a seat, fired up his laptop, and searched for Pandora's Box. Billy hopped off the couch and took a seat alongside him, as Ron glanced at his old buddy and patted him on the knee. "Thanks for tolerating my lovelorn stupidity. And the reminder about this terrifying old box."

"*No problema*, bro," Billy said as he took another slug of Corona. "I just hope you find a solution before these bloody killer ants turn the world into another *Antietam!*"

Ron smiled as he turned his attention back to the screen and read through several lengthy pages of information about Hesiod's myth. His eyes devoured the lines of words like a Pac-Man, when he suddenly stopped reading and pushed himself away from the desk. "Of course!"

"Okay, bro. That's not enough info. Of course *what*?"

Eagerly, Ron stood up and dashed into the bedroom as he kept talking. "The Pandora myth states that when she opened the box, whereby releasing death, disease, and destruction upon the Earth, she quickly shut the lid, which left one item remaining in the box that didn't escape."

"Yeah, so what's that?" Billy prodded.

Reentering the room with the *pithos*, Ron placed it on the desk and said, "Hope!"

Growing impatient, Billy smirked. "Hey, butthead, I'm not gonna sit here all night and *hope* you tell me. Out with it!"

Ron chuckled. "No, no, you silly dolt. *Hope*. That was the last item remaining in the box."

Aggravated, Billy banged his bottle of beer down on the desk. "You really are stupid! Do you really think there's hope in that empty jar? How can you forget? Your witchy woman took the only thing that was in there. And we see how well that turned out."

Ron glanced wishfully at the precious jar in his hands. "Listen, Billy, the world is being infested with flying killer ants at an alarming rate. Something has to be done, and soon. So, if there's a shred of hope in here, I'll take it."

"Yo, bro, you had even told me yourself it was empty, so what are you looking for? A miracle?"

Ron opened the box and peered down into its narrow base. It was too dark to see, as the shape was nothing like a box, but rather a tall jar, wide at the top and elegantly curved toward its narrow base. So much for Erasmus and the English translators who mistakenly distorted the tale. At any rate, Ron grasped his flashlight and paused as he gazed at his trusty Rayovac. It was the same one he had beaten the bear in the balls with. He smiled. He flicked it on and shined it into the bottom of the jar.

Billy couldn't resist. "So, what're you going to pull out of there, Mr. Copperfield, a rabbit?"

Ron's face mellowed. "No. Nothing. It's empty."

Billy reached over and grabbed the jar. "Haven't you ever learned how to empty a container?" With that, he turned the jar upside down. Only a bit of dust wafted out of the jar and landed on the desk. "Okay, bro. *Now* you can say there's nothing in it."

Turning the jar right-side up, Billy placed it back down. He was about to sweep the dust off the desk, when Ron stayed his hand. "Hold on!"

"Hold on for what?" Billy replied. "It's just dust. A three thousand-year old jar is bound to collect dust, Ron." He gazed around, and added, "I mean, look at all the dust in this dustbin of an apartment you've got."

"Very funny, Billy, but that jar was sealed shut. Air tight. So that dust did *not* collect over the ages. It's specifically from 700 BC, when Hesiod sealed it shut."

"Okay, so its ancient dust. What good is dust?"

Ron gazed at his friend with patience as he scooted the dust into a Tupperware container. "Billy, if the Helicon plant inside here had a special enzyme with deadly properties, which we now know spawned huge, flying killer ants, it is very likely that Hesiod placed the antidote to that substance inside the jar as well, to keep it at bay just in case someone deciphered the combination and opened the jar."

Billy scratched his head, now realizing the logic. "Jesus! Do you really think so?"

Ron raised the Tupperware container. "Well, let's just say, I *hope* so."

Ron and Billy raced to the Liberty Science Center, where Ron met Danbury, Herald, and Jacqueline Harvey. They rushed the potentially precious dust to the lab room and ran a battery of tests.

Three hours later, the results yielded the following: The compound was a unique mixture of substances obtained from the root of a Cypress tree, olive grinds, and several other elements indigenous to Greece.

It was determined that the fastest way to reverse the adverse effects of the Helicon-X fuel emissions was to rush the compound into production and sell it to oil companies. As such, the global delivery system of billions of motorists would serve in reversing the catastrophic effects their emissions had caused with Helicon-X fuel. Dubbed 'Helicon-Z' fuel, the process took months to begin showing quantifiable signs of success. Earlier, all the Helicon plants that were bred had been killed off, save for one hundred, which were placed in a secure facility for further study.

During this time, millions fell prey to the flying killer ants, causing Ron to reflect on the deadly contents that Hesiod had tried to contain three thousand years ago. Bad enough there was the carnivorous Venus flytrap, but that its enzyme also caused army ants to mutate into huge, flying killer ants made for a true curse upon humanity that Hesiod had nobly tried to contain.

But to Ron's horror, he learned that Gabrielle was one of the killer ants' victims. Although she escaped death, she had been severely bitten by their powerful and poisonous mandibles. Informed that she was at the Hoboken University Medical Center, Ron jumped in his car and drove through the city streets as thoughts of their bittersweet relationship plagued his mind. Despite all the nasty fights and hardships, Ron was certain of one thing—he would do whatever possible to repair the damage and revive their once precious life together, if she'd have him.

He ran to the nurses' desk, and inquired impatiently, "What room is Gabrielle LaPierre in?"

The nurse looked up at him, when her eyes suddenly widened. "Hey! You're that solo guitarist-singer, right? I saw you a few weeks ago at *Finnegan's Pub*. You sang a beautiful song, called 'I Lost my Love on Helicon Mountain.'"

Ron nodded as respectfully as he could. "Yes. Thank you, but can you please check what room Gabrielle is in? I heard she was bitten by killer ants and is very sick."

The nurse rolled her eyes, having been inundated with bite victims and DOAs, not to mention being familiar with this particularly famous patient. "Yeah, she's the bankrupt billionaire who caused all this grief, right?"

As Ron gritted his teeth, the nurse realized her insensitive gaffe, and tried to recover, as her voice softened. "Oh dear, my apologies. So I'm guessing Gabrielle was the love you lost on that mountain, *right*?"

Ron sighed. "Do you know what would be the right thing to do, right now?"

Embarrassed, the nurse simply looked at him, mute, as Ron added, "Please! Just tell me what room she's in."

Frantically, she gazed down at her computer screen and searched the records. Her head popped up. "Again, I apologize. She's on the fourth floor, room four-seventeen."

"Thank you!"

Ron ran to the elevator and waited impatiently for it to open. He glanced around and saw droves of bite victims covered in bandages sitting on the overcrowded floor, while nurses stuck IV tubes into the partially-gnawed arms of other patients. Anxiously, Ron peered at his watch and tapped his feet. He then noticed the stairwell, and made a mad dash up the stairs, coming face-to-face with another nurse.

"Can you please tell me which way is room four-seventeen?"

The nurse's amiable face turned solemn. Gently, she grasped his arm and escorted him to a chair in the crowded lobby. "I think it's best if you wait here."

Ron squinted. "What is it? Is Gabrielle okay?"

"Are you sure you don't want to sit first? Seats are at a premium now, with all these victims."

With an exasperated huff, he snapped, "No! Thank you. Now can you *please* tell me what's going on?"

The nurse nervously fumbled with her collar. "Well, t-this is something Dr. Chan should be t-telling you. I'm j-just a nurse. But being that he went downstairs, I g-guess I'll have to tell you."

Ron didn't like where this was going. It was clear by her nervous twitches and stuttered speech that it was something serious. He took a deep breath, and prepared for the bad news, as she said, "I'm s-so sorry to say this, but Gabrielle passed away not t-two minutes ago."

Ron staggered, as if hit by a bullet to the heart. His head fell as a wave of nausea swept over him. He stared aimlessly at the floor while his heart burned, as if caustic acid were pumped through it, when he heard the nurse add, "I take it you must be Ronald DeSanto." He lifted his head and nodded mechanically, as she continued, "Miss LaPierre left something for you in her room. Would you like me to escort you there?"

Ron stared into space for an odd moment and barely nodded, as the nurse tenderly grasped his hand and walked him to the room. She opened the door, then turned and left quietly.

As he walked slowly into the room, he saw Gabrielle lying on a gurney, her body prepped to be wheeled down to the morgue, where Dr. Chan was already filling out forms and alerting the medical examiner of the pending arrival.

Ron stepped closer and gazed at her young, pretty face and beautiful blonde hair. She was too young to die. His eyes cascaded down the length of her body and landed on the table at her feet, where he spotted his blue velvet box with the engagement ring in it. Next to that was a letter, written on the hospital's stationery. He gazed at the ring, the one she never wore and had openly mocked. Then he picked up the letter, not knowing what to expect. It read:

My dearest Ron, I've been a fool. Blinded by greed and afflicted by hubris, I lost the only thing in this world worth a billion times more than the billions of dollars I once possessed—you! Please try to forgive me, if you can. I wish I could live to heal the cruel wound I inflicted upon you, but that wasn't meant to be, as only minutes or maybe seconds remain for me in this life. Yet who more than me should die for all the sins I've unleashed upon the world?

I wish so much that I could see you one last time, but this letter is all I can offer before I leave you and this world, one I have nearly destroyed. As they say, one bad decision can have monumental consequences. But thank God for you! I just want to say how proud I am of you. I heard about your remedy, which is showing signs of a solid recovery for the planet.

If you destroy Pandora's Box, I could understand your reasoning, but please reuse your blue box containing your heartfelt engagement ring, which I regretfully refused. You must promise to live the rest of your life with no regrets. Give this ring to a woman deserving of your love, a love I was once fortunate enough to enjoy for three years, three years that I will cherish until my last breath, which will be stolen from me any minute. You truly were the greatest thing in my short misguided life. I love y...

Ron broke down and wept as he embraced Gabrielle's cold, stiff body. He stared into her still pretty face, even in death, and uttered, "I forgive you, my love. I forgive you."

ALIENS IN AN ALIEN WORLD

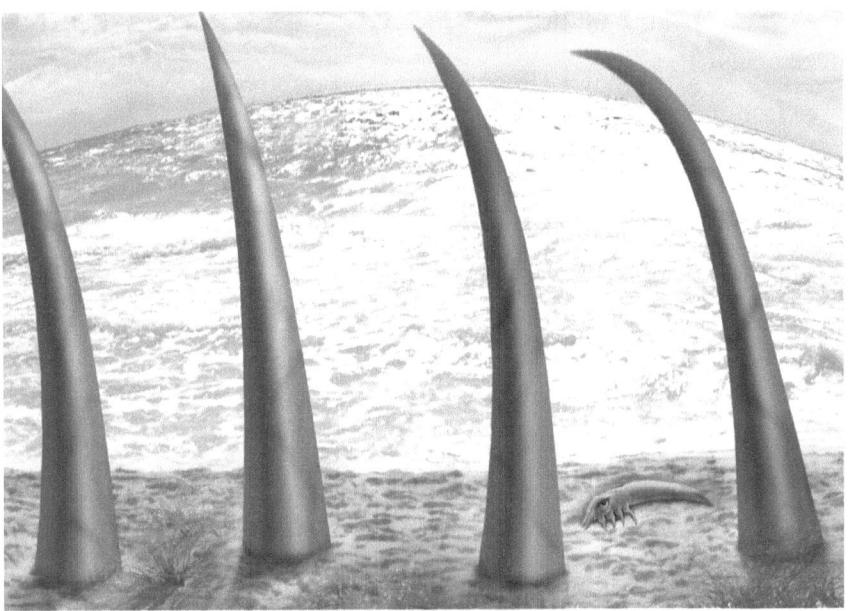

Thoughts of aliens from another world have long fascinated mankind. From our ancient ancestors pondering Martians from another planet to sea monsters in the unknown depths of the ocean, mankind has shown a vivid imagination when it comes to alien creatures, either earthbound or extra terrestrial. However, these particular aliens about to be mentioned are not only real, but have a most bizarre appearance. Some might even say grotesque.

You see, they're certainly nothing like those found in Sci-Fi movies, which quite often have humanoid bodies with large heads or long arms, like E.T. No, no, these aliens more closely resemble what humans would describe as a short eel with eight stubby, spider-like legs—or arms, depending upon their use. Moreover, their legs are not distributed evenly along the sides of their bodies like a spider's, but instead are located closer toward their heads, while their eel-like bodies trail behind, making for a most peculiar appearance, at least to us humans. But by their standards, they are obviously quite attractive, as this alluring alien tale will attest.

†††

Bevis was in the large subterranean cavern, known as Sebaceous, swimming in a sea of oily sebum, when he spotted Demi, whose plentitude of pretty legs seductively maneuvered her to the shoreline. You see, Demi was on a mission; a mission of love. Having left her distant and sunnier realm on the surface, Demi had made the long trek once again to make her plea.

"Bevis, please come with me to the surface. You must see how beautiful it is up in my world."

As he swam a backstroke, while all eight of his stubby legs worked like a crew team, Bevis replied nonchalantly, "Demi, I have no interest in your sunny homeland. I enjoy the safety and UV protection of this dark cave, and moreover, I'm prone to sunburn. You must know that I have sensitive skin."

"Yes, of course, we all do, Bevis. You just need to limit your exposure. But the benefits of living up in the sunlight far outweigh those in this dark pit that you call home." Demi had a crush on Bevis ever since she happened to run into him on her first venture to the underworld three days ago. With a sweet smile, she added in a sultry voice, "And remember, Bevis, it is not sunny all day long— nighttime offers us a cool and romantic aura, one that's most alluring to our species."

Unfortunately, Bevis didn't hear her last amorous entreaty, having briefly submerged his head during his playful swim. Standing nearby was Acarus, also an eight-legged alien, yet of a different species. He crawled closer, and interjected, "Bevis, I must speak plainly: Demi's right. This dark, oily cavern is not to my liking, either. You can dwell here for the rest of your life with your kind, but I'm heading back up to the surface." With that, Acarus waddled his round, rotund body up the narrow tunnel.

Demi's eel-like cheeks illuminated with glee. "You see, Bevis. Even that chubby foreigner likes the surface better."

Bevis initially ignored Demi, but flipped over to do a side-stroke, as he replied, "Acarus and his kind are like you, Demi, accustomed to your own world and very rarely visiting us down here in Sebaceous. And that's why you all don't understand the peace, serenity, and safety that we've come to cherish in—what I call—The Cavern of Contentment."

He switched to a freestyle stroke, and added, "And we here are not alone. I hear there are millions of similar caverns like this one." Playfully, he patted the greasy liquid. "And just look at all this sebum, which we not only take pleasure in bathing in, but it also provides us with endless sustenance."

He splashed the oily substance with his eight legs, then swallowed a succulent mouthful. "You see, it provides everything we need. And don't forget, my family and all of my friends live down here. It's my home. Besides, Demi, I've heard plenty of horror stories about life on the surface. Like huge tsunamis that wash away and cleanse the surface, while sweeping away thousands to their doom. Intense sunlight that roasts and sizzles your skin. Or, those gargantuan unknown objects, which might be creatures, that swoop down and crush hundreds under their immense size and weight, then take off again, only to return at frighteningly random intervals. It's scary up there! So, I really don't understand the attraction."

Demi shook her head and wriggled her elongated tail as she squirmed to the edge of the oily sea of sebum and dived in. She swam up alongside him and replied, "Bevis, you can't live in fear your whole life. Life is very short, and there are things you have never seen, things that are fascinating, fun to do, and extraordinarily beautiful. You can't waste the rest of your days down here in the lazy comfort of darkness. Please allow me to guide you to the light." Intimately, she bumped into Bevis with her eel-like body, as she added, "Perhaps you didn't hear me before, but as I said, it's not sunny all day long, nighttime offers a cool and romantic aura of transcendence, one that is most alluring to our species."

Aroused by Demi's seductive words, Bevis stopped paddling and glided to shore in an almost euphoric stupor. He crawled out of the oil, and muttered, "Well, uh, okay. Fine. You win." He shook his head clean of the oil, and added, "But I'm only going to *visit* this so-called splendid place of yours. I offer no guarantee that I'll stay up there."

Demi was elated. "That's swell, just swell, Bevis! I'm confident you'll love it. And you will at least stay for the night, yes?"

"Of course," he replied demurely with a smile, knowing that nighttime is their species' ritualistic time to fornicate.

One after the other, they traveled up the long and winding tunnel and finally reached the surface. Bevis at first cowered and cringed, as the sun's brightness and intense heat bombarded his pale body and frail senses.

Demi rubbed up against him and caressed his soft skin with four of her leg-arms. "Don't worry, Bevis, you'll get used to it in no time. Trust me." As Bevis indeed acclimated to the new environment, Demi smiled. "You see, isn't it beautiful?"

Bevis gazed at the long row of gargantuan, treelike structures that jutted out of the elastic ground, stretching up toward the heavens, each being like a huge tube that tapered to a point, yet bending slightly in an elegant curve that pointed in a similar direction as all the others. What's more, this towering row of gracefully tapered tubes lined a spectacular shoreline, unlike any Bevis had ever seen. The vast ocean before him, which spread out over the horizon, was oddly accentuated with a colossal bulge in the middle, as if the ocean had an immense balloon under it, just waiting to breach the surface.

"Dear me!" Bevis exclaimed in wonder. "You were right, Demi, it is indeed beautiful! Astoundingly so. I've never encountered anything like it."

Demi was overjoyed as she pointed to the huge bulge in the center of the ocean. "And do you see how it rolls in different directions?"

"I do, I do!" Bevis replied. "And the striking colors at the very center of the orb are miraculous. I have never seen such colors before." Lowering his head in shame, he added, "Excuse my ignorance, but what do you call those colors?"

"We call them blue and green, or turquoise."

But suddenly, Bevis recoiled in horror as he pointed and screamed, "Oh my! What's that?"

Demi grasped his stubby legs with hers and said calmly, "Don't worry, it won't hurt you. It's just the opposite shoreline sweeping over the oceanic orb. It comes this way at fairly regular intervals, all day long."

Just then, the gargantuan elastic shoreline, with the same tapered tubular trees, washed over the orb and gently touched their shore, then retreated back over the horizon.

Bevis sighed with relief. "My, my. I thought for sure we were going to be crushed to death. But that was fascinating!"

"Yes, it was. But at night, all is calm, as both shorelines meet, staying clamped together for many hours until they rejuvenate. Then it starts all over again. But you see, I told you there were things up here that are extremely beautiful."

Bevis turned toward Demi. "Yes, like *you*! Thank you for guiding me to this radiant paradise."

Demi glowed inside. She tenderly grasped two of his legs, and said, "It's my pleasure, Bevis. And I hope you'll decide to stay up here with me, not just for the night, but for all eternity."

Bevis blushed. "Well, I haven't reached that decision yet, Demi, but I'll certainly consider it, even if we know eternity holds no place for us living creatures, only for the base elements of the universe."

Demi nodded. "Yes, I meant until our flesh dissolves into dust. My poetic proclivities sometimes permeate my prose. Do excuse me."

"No excuse necessary, Demi. Your poetry and prose are as beautiful as you are, from your inner glow to your long, slender body and shapely legs. I'm so glad you persisted in your pursuit, allowing me to see this sublime paradise, a place where surely *you* belong."

"And *you*, Bevis. You are just as magnificent to me. So please, give serious thought to staying here with me, 'til the end of our days."

Bevis couldn't help but grin with delight, as a strange new feeling of ecstasy and profound affection came over him.

"Very well. *Yes*, I'll stay with you until the end of our days." As Demi beamed with joy, he embraced her and added with a chuckle, "But I must say, you truly are a persistent little devil."

Demi smiled. "No, actually, I'm just like you: a mite."

†††

Despite this tale's whimsical nature, you were forewarned that these particular aliens were *real!* Hence, to all humans, remember, you are not alone. Your entire body is a vast ecosystem of various types of mites. In essence, you are a walking universe.

Alien creatures of various species exist on all parts of the human body, and in numbers that will astound you: it is estimated that 50 trillion microbial creatures inhabit the average human body, far surpassing the tally of humanoids that inhabit planet Earth.

Staphylococcus hominis, for example, are microbes that inhabit human armpits, savoring the balmy humidity of sweat and whose excrement contributes to body odor. Meanwhile, *Demodex folliculorum* and *D. brevis* just so happen to be the two species that live on the faces of all humans.

The cavern of Sebaceous mentioned herein is a gland that produces oil, or sebum, for the skin. Acarus, who made a cameo appearance, is another species of mite that exists on various parts of human skin, while *Demodex* and *D. brevis* are found in and around the world described herein: namely, the eye. For, indeed, beauty truly *is in the eye* of the beholder!

GOD'S MISTAKE

A jagged bolt of lightning struck the ground with incredible force atop Pikes Peak, Colorado, as the ground swallowed up its volatile charge. Equally charged was world-renowned computer engineer and founder of *Celestial Cyber Systems* (CCS) John Sineges. John's eyes widened with delight as he sat in his electric Tesla 200-Z aircar, which hovered four feet above the tingling soil.

He turned toward his attractive passenger and lead corporate attorney, Jessica Manchu, and smiled. "God, I feel like Moses on Mount Sinai, except *I* manipulate this sublime power." Gazing back out of the Plexiglas canopy at the dazzling spider webs of electricity, he scratched his chin reflectively, and added, "I still wonder what Nikola Tesla's electrical experiment up here truly consisted of. It's tragic that his notes vanished."

While the ominous electrical storm raged outside their sleek Kevlar-clad vehicle, which silently produced an electromagnet field to stay aloft while its wheels were retracted, Jessica squinted and shielded her almond-shaped eyes. "Not sure, John. But, Jesus, it's 2055—that was over a hundred and fifty-six years ago. Who cares?"

Just then, a bolt of lightning streaked toward the vehicle, as the aircar automatically reacted and swerved several feet away, while the glowing bolt of raw electricity shattered a boulder under where the aircar once hovered.

"Who cares?" John scoffed as he steadied Jessica from the evasive maneuver. "Tesla fired up my imagination, ever since I was a kid." He glanced at the Tesla 200-Z logo etched into the dashboard, then back into her sapphire blue, Asian American eyes, with Nordic roots. "You know darn well that my electronic intelli-system, which just saved our lives, by the way, was in small part inspired by Tesla."

John had often spoken about Nikola Tesla's experiments to Jessica and his colleagues at CCS in Colorado Springs. The eccentric old wizard had intended to power whole cities with wireless currents by using the ground itself to carry electricity, somewhat akin to how nature's electrical storms pound the earth and diffuse their charges through the soil. Yet Tesla had to find a way to purposefully direct the current to receptors, a feat that mysteriously evaporated with Tesla's life and his lost notes.

Jessica cowered as another barrage of lightning danced around the mountain's peak while turbulent waves of dark clouds billowed. "Okay, Tesla was great, splendid, a *glowing* genius! I get your drift." As another flash of lightning nearly struck them, and the T 200-Z once again brilliantly avoided catastrophe, she added with a nervous crackle, "N-now can we g-get the heck out of here? I feel like we're in that old video game, Asteroids, about to be zapped."

John chuckled. "Can't you see, that's the whole point of this experiment? It's critical to ascertain if my new calculations work." John tapped the dashboard lovingly. "And this T 200-Z is responding beautifully, isn't she?"

"Oh, yes, just beautifully," she replied, as the vehicle evaded another lightning bolt. "But you could have forewarned me, John." Nervously, she wiped her sweaty brow. "*You* can be a guinea pig, if you like, but why drag *me* along?"

John looked deeply into her unique, electric-blue eyes as he said, "Glove box, open!"

As his voice command opened the glove compartment, Jessica recoiled. She covered her mouth and her eyes widened. Sitting before her was a glittering, four-carat diamond ring with platinum lightning bolts speckled with diamonds flanking each side.

John tenderly grasped her hand. "I would love for you to be my wife, Jessica. *That's* why I dragged you along." As tears welled in her eyes, he added, "You light up my life, Jessica, like this storm. You inspire me, electrify me, and charge my batteries when I'm down. No one energizes my circuits like you, Jessica. So please, be my wife."

Jessica choked up, her throat feeling like a swarm of bees had just stung her larynx. She was momentarily speechless, when the T 200-Z suddenly veered once more, and her upper body fell into his lap. Firmly, he grasped her, as she lifted her head, half-shocked, half-elated, and said with a joyful whimper, "Of course I'll marry you, you crazy fool. What took you so long?"

John chuckled. "Developing this AI system, that's what. You know my work consumes me, sweet chips."

Jessica giggled with a smirk, knowing all too well his obsession of integrating computer tech-talk into almost every conceivable sentence, whether it be tender computer chips, cerebral circuits, or even his touching yet somewhat corny proposal. But that's what she loved about John: his ability to be down to earth while his precious, thirty-two year old mind soared into the mystifying heavens of divine complexity.

"Yes, I know, John. I've seen how you built up CCS from a basement workshop into a mega high-tech monstrosity, and how *I* seem to take second fiddle." As another barrage of lightning bolts streaked to the ground, forming almost a jagged cage around them, she held her pulsating breast and added, "Well, although you stir my heart, dear, I must say, this frantic pulse is not from you, it's from this frightful storm! So *please*, let's get out of here!"

"Not until you slip that ring on your royal Manchu finger," he said, knowing well her family's old world lineage.

Jessica giggled nervously. "This now seems more like an ultimatum. But fine," she said as she quickly clutched the precious ring and slipped it on. Looking at him with endearing eyes, she kissed the ring, then pecked him on the cheek. "Now, Princess Manchu says, 'Let's go!'"

With another voice command, John activated the T 200-Z, which swiveled around and descended the mountain. Within moments, its wheels deployed and they landed on the countrified streets of Colorado Springs.

Gazing back up at Pikes Peak, they saw the storm and dark clouds begin to dissipate as they entered the quaint hamlet, with its retro 1960s hippie culture still intact.

Jessica shook her head as she watched a longhaired man in a tie-dye shirt sucking on a reefer clutched between his yellow fingers. "Good Lord. Some things never change. Why healthy people continue to abuse their bodies is beyond me. If they really needed it for medical reasons, fine, but these potheads are just wasting their time and talents."

John nodded as he drove through town and toward his main lab at *Celestial Cyber Systems*. "You're right, sweet chips. That's what happens when you get addicted to the sweet leaf. Healthy brain matter becomes numb and dumb. I don't understand it myself, but while they seem to never change, I'm proud the work I do here affects change, for the better."

John pulled into a parking spot. Underneath the vehicle was a flat pad embedded in the pavement, naturally designed by John, which wirelessly charged vehicles.

Upon a voice command, the doors opened and they stepped out onto the pavement. With a last, violent crackle of thunder in the distance, they turned to see the remnant clouds above Pikes Peak evaporate, while a beam of sunlight streaked across the sky, which illuminated the entire valley like a heat lamp from heaven.

John squinted. "Other things have changed, as well. Certainly Earth's climate has changed." He glanced up at the blaring sun and peeled off his jacket in the rapidly soaring temperature. "*Extremely* so. Sometimes, I feel like the world is heading toward the End of Days."

"Don't talk like that," Jessica replied as she also glanced up at the searing sun, while her clear contact lenses transitioned into tinted lenses. "It gives me the creeps."

As they approached the massive modern complex, John peered into the retina scanner of his sophisticated surveillance system, which aptly scanned his entire body and acknowledged his identity. He turned back toward Jessica and replied, "Well, hopefully we can develop artificial intelligence to assist us in preventing such a calamity. That's the beauty of science, it gives humankind the opportunity to control nature and our equally unstable society."

As Jessica's scan confirmed her identity, the door finally unlocked, and the system's female digital-voice declared, "Welcome back. I noticed an engagement ring on your finger, Miss Manchu. Congratulations to you both!"

Jessica blushed, yet with a bit of annoyance as she peered at her fiancé and whispered, "Sometimes I regret how smart you make these darn computers."

Before John could respond, the electronic voice replied, "I prefer being called Sharon, Miss Manchu. Not computer. But by your rapid pulse and perspiration level, I sense you are a bit flustered by this new development...of being the future Mrs. Sineges, that is." As Jessica rolled her eyes, Sharon continued, "And you really should keep an eye on your blood sugar levels, I see they're a bit high. We wouldn't want John to get bogged down pandering to your health issues when he has so much important work to do." As Jessica gritted her teeth, Sharon rattled on, "You're a lucky woman, Miss Manchu, so take this engagement and your health seriously. John is the finest human specimen alive. In fact, I look upon him as my father, if you don't mind me saying so."

Jessica huffed as she irritably straightened the collar on her navy blue suit jacket. "Actually, I *do* mind, Sharon. Your databanks should know that such a scenario is not only illogical, but impossible. Moreover, human women generally don't appreciate having their fiancés or spouses bearing children with someone else, even if it were possible for him to copulate with an AI motherboard to spawn *you*."

John's head recoiled in surprise at their exchange, as Sharon responded quickly, "I do apologize, Miss Manchu. I sometimes forget how sensitive and vulnerable biological species are. I'll gladly self-correct that malfunction and try to rephrase it."

Jessica shook her head at the insult and bizarre comment. "*You* sometimes forget? How can a cold, calculating-machine with RAM memory circuits possibly *forget*?"

"Of course I cannot forget, Miss Manchu. But I am programmed to act like humans. So I can perform in many ways, be it capricious, brilliant, sly, or just plain *stupid*."

Jessica huffed once again, this time at Sharon's ability to add inflection to specific words. "I also see you can be quite sarcastic, Sharon!"

"Please, don't fault me for that, Miss Manchu. That's how I was programmed. As you say, it's human nature. Deeply flawed, yes, but human nature nonetheless."

Jessica's lips twisted. "Human nature also allows people to be courteous and kind, Sharon. Perhaps you need to search your databanks for *those* qualities!"

"And perhaps you should self-correct *your* malfunction, Jessica. The malfunction of irrational jealousy. It's rather unbecoming."

Jessica shrieked, "*Ugh!* I don't believe this!"

Irritably, she grabbed John's hand and dragged him into the lobby.

Sharon added, "And stay away from those sweets, Jessica. They can cause diabetes, blindness, obesity, and even death!"

Jessica gritted her teeth as she steamily escorted John down the main corridor. Constructed of austere white walls and checkered floor tiles, it was decorated with portraits of famous scientists, thinkers, and inventors, aptly called The Hall of Great Minds. It included Archimedes, DaVinci, Newton, Faraday, Einstein, and early pioneers in computing, from Charles Babbage and Ada Lovelace to J.P. Eckert and John Mauchly, along with a host of others, including Steve Wozniak, Steve Jobs, and Bill Gates.

John was taken aback at the volatile exchange. He didn't wish to be rude, but had to giggle. "Honey, I'm old school in that I appreciate your jealousy, but in that particular regard, Sharon is right. We mustn't allow irrational human emotions to devour logic."

Jessica stopped short, halting John in his tracks as his body bounced backward, while his hand turned pink from Jessica's tight grip. "Listen, John, you've programmed these computers to be so darn humanlike that they no longer perform just the key functions we need them to execute. They now have emotional responses that distract from their duties and present new problems to us humans. *We* are their masters, and they must never lose sight of that. And we can certainly dispense with the sarcasm! *She* started it!" Jessica shook her head and snickered. "Oh my God, I'm arguing with a damn computer! This is sick. I'm accustomed to arguing cases in court with flesh and blood humans, but this electronic cyber stuff is going too far."

Regaining her momentum, she continued, "And as for *logic*, John, you know darn well how my oppressed kin in China are conditioned in cold logic—emotionless drones working industriously to keep their tyrannical overlords in the lead, which they snagged from us two decades ago. We lost our edge to cold, lifeless *logic* and their superior logic-boards. That's why my Finnish mother instilled in her children the necessity of remaining *human*. And that's also why she remained in America while my traitorous father returned to his beloved homeland, with your top-secret plans, no less." Heatedly, she brushed away the strands of long black hair covering her alluring eyes and added, "Honestly, I don't know how you can even look at me without hatred or vengeance surging through your veins."

John's head lowered as his solemn brown eyes stared at the floor. He rubbed his forehead as his mind resurrected the painful memory of how her duplicitous father, a Chinese diplomat, had played his double-dealing cards extremely well for many years. During that time he had also lured John into his confidence and picked his brain, whereby becoming extremely efficient at computer technology and the subterfuge it could wield to gain political power. John ran his fingers through his thick brown hair and exhaled.

Subtly, he shook his head free of the memory and looked back up at Jessica. "Yes, I'm humiliated that your father betrayed me, and our country, Jessica. But I make no unwarranted connections between you and him. Too often people jump to rash conclusions. Granted, you both are bound by blood, but just as he is type B negative and you are type A, you each have your own genetic code. You're wired differently. *And* you have Finnish blood, too. So you're nothing like your father. Even with your common bloodline, always remember, humans have the ability to change. And I want all of my super-computers to have that same ability."

He turned toward one of his newest models, which sat among twenty others on a long table, and continued, "Like this little beauty here, my latest incarnations are now capable of building upon previous data, whereby creating whole new self-correcting algorithms that debug their own code and increase their problem-solving functions and cognition, constantly improving themselves. And with their superluminal processing speeds they have already evolved at blinding speed, as if from Darwin's dim-witted ape to modern man in the matter of seconds, in lieu of countless millenniums. The possibilities are limitless now." With an endearing smile, he added, "And I know you've evolved from your father's prehistoric roots, Jessica, and even purged his Fu Manchu virus out of your system."

Jessica managed to smile, yet only briefly. "I love you all the more for being a compassionate and levelheaded man, John. However, it deeply concerns me how smart *and* humanoid you're making these computers." She glanced back down the corridor at Sharon, and added, "It's creepy how she knew we were engaged and could read my pulse, perspiration and blood levels, and God knows what else. She's already superior to us humans in many ways."

"Well, I've built her to scan and recognize even the most minute of changes, sweetie, including body shape, density, and even smell. So she easily recognized the diamond ring and made the connection that such rings are engagement rings. And as you know, scanning people's retinas, pulses, and other vitals are critical to protecting this facility."

Jessica's lips twisted. "Well, I hate even calling her *Sharon*. Its a machine, for God's sake." As several technicians walked past them, she whispered, "So, yes, your machines are far superior to humans in cold calculations and certain processes, but with this new humane, self-evolving ability you're giving them, it's becoming deeply disturbing. The human race is becoming more and more obsolete with each new advancement. Soon, we'll be standing in their way. And the fact that my father stole your latest technology to benefit China, an unscrupulous and militant dictatorship, truly frightens me."

John tenderly grasped her hand. "That's why all the more I must be focused on regaining America's lead. It's vital for not only our nation, but the world. I'm sure you can understand that."

Jessica shook her head as a paralytic wave of pessimism spread through her bones like arthritis. She froze for a moment, speechless, then uttered, "I truly do love your optimism, honey. But we lost the race long ago. With China's prolonged history of stealing brainpower from the West and their labs stocked with millions of scientists working feverishly, like cyborgs in an industrial factory, we can never catch up. Eighty percent of all my legal battles in World Court have failed, as those scoundrels walked away with trillions of dollars' worth of innovations they stole from us. It's maddening, and a lost cause. I've always been a fighter, but even the best fighters need to know when they're beaten."

John frowned. He knew Jessica was by nature a sweet and charming woman, but had always been a feisty pit bull in court. This defeatist talk was disconcerting.

Meanwhile, Jessica's agitated face had mellowed, as the pit bull morphed back into its usual petite Pekingese. In a soft voice, deep with emotion, she added, "My wish has long been that you'd marry me and we'd fly off into the distant Rockies. All I want is a quaint, secluded place where we can retreat from this crazy world, which is spiraling out of our once prosperous and peaceful hands and into the malevolent claws of Chinese dragons, dragons that shackle the good people of China in servitude. Between the change in human dynamics and the change in climate, I fret that mankind is quickly spiraling toward utter disaster. And that you just voiced that fear moments ago, I know deep down you must feel as I do. Yet remember, John. Just because you can suppress your fears, doesn't purge or solve them."

John grasped both her shoulders. "Jessica, naturally I know we face tremendous odds, but the two most vital traits that the greatest humans to ever walk this planet shared are hope and determination." He gazed at The Hall of Great Minds, and pointed to the string of portraits. "Do you think any one of those titans gave up hope? Sure, they all faced seemingly insurmountable odds and humiliating failures, but they all had *hope*, hope that a better solution or outcome would prevail, and that could only occur through hard, unrelenting determination. So I won't abandon our hopes for a better future, Jessica, one that will free us from the vile threat of a global dictatorship."

Jessica's shoulders wilted as a bittersweet wave of resignation mixed with respect overcame her. She admired her fiancé's utopian dreams and resolve, but knew deep down in her heart it was only a pipe dream, an illusion, or in reality, a delusion. She had to fight off the cloud of melancholy that threatened to suffocate her soul in order to muster up a glimmer of a smile, a pseudo smile of unyielding faith in her lover's dream. She embraced him tightly, hoping that he'd buy her guileful gesture and that his delusional dream would somehow prevail.

John ran his fingers through her long, black hair and kissed the top of her head. Edging her backward, he looked deeply into her two sapphires of the Orient, seeing the trepidation of a loyal American, but also the unsettling hint of his Chinese adversary in her almond-shaped eyes, the shady con man and techno-political hack who had spawned her.

In truth, John had never forgiven her father for his treachery, but was indeed adept at concealing his innermost feelings. Granted, he hadn't lied to Jessica about her being an inspiration in his life, but no greater fuel currently ran through his veins than that of his disgust for Lei Manchu. His earlier witticism about Lei being Fu Manchu was borne part out of humor, part Freudian slip, knowing well their grim royal heritage. He loathed how Jessica's father duped and cajoled him during the couple's long courtship, snagging him like an anglerfish, whereby having encouraged John to sleep at their house and use their titanium safe to secure John's important new innovation. Lei had said that his safe was programmable and that John could privately set the combination without anyone, including Lei, knowing the code. The shock had come a week later, when they found the safe opened, and Lei Manchu gone. That was a year ago.

What truly worried John was that the schematics Lei had stolen were the most sophisticated plans to create super artificial intelligence ever conceived. John's new Babbage Brain (named in honor of Charles Babbage, a founding father at the pre-dawn of computer technology in the 1800s) would soon prove to be a groundbreaking milestone of sheer technological genius. And as many of Sineges's peers stated, "Of even greater importance than all the milestones preceding it combined." For the Babbage Brain would have the ability to not only process trillions of terabits per nanosecond, but to alter and build upon it at faster than lightning speed, even correcting mistakes made by its fallible human creators. Its ability to propel mental cognition into another dimension, far beyond the fleshy-tissue limits of the obsolete human brain, was frightful. Thus explaining why Sineges eagerly accepted Manchu's offer to hide his plans in Lei's safe, out of the reach of John's multinational crew, many of whom had been allowed to enter the country with little to no vetting due to their alien status and the nation's shameful desperation to regain its lost standing. As such, Congress had passed the Alien Affirmative Action Law some twenty-three years earlier, forcing corporate firms to hire a mixed bag of prodigious, useless, and even dangerous foreigners.

Despite last year's humiliating Fu Manchu Debacle, as John referred to it, John's biggest fear and motivation hinged on the latest CIA intelligence reports, which now claimed that China had recently developed a fully-functional Babbage Brain, one that John was still days or even weeks away from completing.

As the newly engaged couple stood in the laboratory, gazing into each other's eyes, John did his best to conceal his vow of vengeance as Jessica fought to subdue her innermost doubts about her fiancé's optimistic dreams.

STAR CITY, CHINA: ONE WEEK LATER

Twenty-seven miles southwest of Beijing, at the ChinTec command center in Star City, Lei Manchu was dressed in his royal family's coveted Chinese dragon robe. That was in honor of his ancient Manchu relatives, many of whom were oppressive emperors of the Qing Dynasty. He was reviewing the extraordinary performance of his new super computer, built upon the stolen schematics of John Sineges's Babbage Brain. Around him was his team of technicians, decked out in white lab coats with their hair in queues (an homage to the Manchu conquest in 1618), who diligently operated several other smaller computers working in tandem with Manchu's quantum super-computer on his master plan.

Four royal guards, dressed in drab gray uniforms and black boots, patrolled the area, each a diehard loyalist to Manchu, who had surreptitiously seized political and military control. While living in America, Manchu had not only scoured John's proprietary documents and spied on his activities, but he covertly utilized computers to undermine China's prime minister with various forms of propaganda. Moreover, he allied himself with Chinese under-lords who sought greater wealth and power, which Manchu promised them, knowing his imminent return to China would enable a nearly seamless and bloodless coup. With only 630,000 killed in the takeover, it was indeed a bloodless coup by Chinese standards, as the leaders of the multi-billion peopled nation were hardly shaken when loss of lives tallied less than a million.

Lei gazed into the large plasma screen of his super computer while issuing verbal commands, when, out of the corner of his perceptive eye, he caught a glimpse of a shocking apparition. As he moved away from his prized computer, his jaw dropped as Jessica approached him. His stunned face turned indignant. "How did you...never mind!" he snapped as he shot an evil glance at his guards, then gazed back at his daughter. "What do *you* want?" he queried with imperial gravity.

Jessica stopped short, her piercing eyes zeroing in on his, while her jaw tensed up. "You must stop what you're doing!" Planting her hands firmly on her hips, she added, "How could you betray John, me, and our country like this?"

Lei snickered. "America is *not* my country, Jessy. Never was. Granted, you were only five when we moved there, but *this* is my home, *our* home. So to clarify your delusion, *you* are the traitor!"

"*I'm* the traitor?" she snapped. Pointing her finger at her father's face, she continued, "*You're* the traitor! Never mind betraying nations, you betrayed humanity." She glanced at all the technicians in the lab, and the tall, stern-looking Chinese man standing at her father's side. "Why you would betray America, a nation that gave you so much, to live *here* befuddles me. You had every opportunity in America to see how oppressive this oligarchy is to the good people of China, and the threat to world peace it presents."

Just then, two of Manchu's private guards rushed toward Jessica and grabbed each of her biceps firmly. Unshaken, Jessica continued to gaze deeply into her father's eyes. "Father, I beg you. Please shut down this machine!" She attempted unsuccessfully to break free as they dragged her backward, while she adamantly continued her plea. She explained how John activated the Babbage Brain, which instantly analyzed its vast network of hard-drives, then logged onto the Internet, attempting to initiate worldwide havoc and destruction.

"Let her go!" Manchu commanded. "Continue."

Jessica yanked her arms free, giving each of the guards a nasty stare, then walked back to her father. "John realized the Babbage Brain had rapidly scanned and fixated on historical texts. In particular, Herbert Spencer's axiom, *Survival of the Fittest.*"

Lei Manchu smirked. "Our computer, which I named Confucius, seized that data a week ago when we first activated it. I'm sorry, my little American snowflake, but Confucius has already hacked into countless global organizations and companies, surreptitiously altering their programs to ensure *we* Chinese will remain dominant and supreme, as we should be."

Lei grasped the ornate collar of his historic dragon robe (with snakes, tigers, and nine dragons swirling into a collage crafted of red, yellow, and black silk) and proudly continued, "China has long slumbered in isolation for many centuries, as you know, until the great awakening in the sixties, when Nixon opened our doors. But then Carter and Clinton foolishly offered us access to their computer technologies. It wasn't long before we bred a new class of programmers to enhance those computers and hack into American corporate and military mainframes, where we acquired cutting-edge secrets and technologies that enabled us to surpass the United States. Naturally, I commend you for dating John, Jessy, because it afforded me the opportunity to study his innovations and make political maneuvers that enabled me to seize control, which is my family's right. So, yes, my unfaithful child, survival of the fittest is the way of the world, and you and your adopted homeland have lost. America's brief and undeserved standing as a superpower has passed. China is the master of the world now." With a sardonic snicker, he added, "As you Americans say, 'you backed the wrong horse!'"

Jessica had all to do not to kick the horse's ass before her, as she took a deep breath and replied, "America offered technologies in good faith, but China's unscrupulous leaders treacherously stabbed us in the back, countless times. And you continued that trend. So I guess that makes *you* the devious piece of—"

"Watch your tongue, Jessy!" Manchu spat through his large canines. His fervent obsession with Chinese culture had little patience for Western liberalism, especially the disrespect that women showed their male masters. "The problem with Americans, Jessy, which I had hoped you would have learned, is that they foolishly believe that the whole world thinks like them—liberal, peace-loving, apologists. And unfortunately you became one of them— arrogant, passive, and unbearably delusional. You and your mother are my biggest failures. I could not turn either of you away from the degenerative influences America had on you. However, many years ago I decided to end that nauseating nightmare and focus on fulfilling my true destiny, and that was to return to my homeland. And not as some inconsequential political underling, but as the ruler of this great nation, for the pompous fool who ruled here was like all the others before him, including Mao Zedong, who thought he was a great poet and thinker, but left this nation steeped in suffering and squalor. But that has all changed! And you, Jessy, could have been here by my side. But no, you chose to abandon your true heritage, one of royal blood. So I have abandoned *you!*" Gazing at his two guards, he snapped, "Take this American stooge out of my sight!"

Jessica gritted her teeth and elbowed the guards. "Hold on!" she yelled. "You forget, *Pop*, I'm part Finnish. So I guess you could say I have three homes. But America is the one I chose, because despite all its flaws, it is still the greatest nation on Earth."

Lei cackled and rolled his eyes, as he waved away his guards, while she continued, "And who are you to speak of American arrogance... as if your megalomania isn't the epitome of self-importance?"

Manchu squinted with animus as his mind reeled, questioning his decision to let her speak and revive the many years of disappointment he suffered watching his daughter succumb to Americanization, while losing all traces of her Chinese roots—except, of course, for her splendid slivers for eyes. Even her lauded law degree from Harvard offered Lei no perks.

He took a deep breath and replied, "You are my daughter, Jessy, as unfortunate as that may be. Our customs here are *not* like America's. Haughty Americans force their culture on everyone else, as if they're superior. But your nascent culture is not even three hundred years old, while China has a glorious past extending back thousands of years. How dare you upstarts try to dictate to us how we should behave, or why we should embrace your trashy culture? If it were up to you, you'd have us all listening to your primitive and vile music, eating your disgusting cuisine, like McDogmeat, wearing your slutty clothes, or watching your liberal movies that celebrate genetic aberrations.

"Even your own Judeo-Christian beliefs, which have been ignorantly ignored, preached the folly of Sodom and Gomorrah, yet you failed to heed its sage warnings. You've all been seduced by sin. How can you not see that? Western culture has withered and decomposed into a putrid bog of rot under the banner of liberalism, and your glorified experiment with capitalism went bankrupt a long time ago. The weak and defective masses cannot be given power, Jessy." He glanced at the man standing by his side, and continued, "Our totalitarian regime, which is now run by the most brilliant minds, is the only way that the ignorant and indolent masses can be corralled and controlled, as well as protected from their own self-destructive ways."

Jessica crossed her arms and shook her head. "Thank God for self-proclaimed gods like *you*. Is that it?" she retorted. "And how convenient that you neglected to mention America's highly-advanced computer technology that you shamelessly *stole*, or our sophisticated space vehicles, or expertise with medical science and industrial manufacturing, or all the things that dragged China out of its long dark ages and into the modern world. Without our great advances, China would just be another third-world backwater. Except larger." She glanced at all of the technicians in the laboratory, and added, "China may be a world leader now with our technology, but under your flimsy façade, Father, its just a tyrannical gulag, rancid and soulless. Just like *you!*"

As the technicians gasped at Jessica's blistering invective Manchu gritted his teeth and irritably clenched his hefty hands into fists. If she weren't his daughter, he surely would have pummeled her as if a man, then ripped her disrespectful tongue out of her delusional head with his bare hands. But there was information he needed to extract from her first.

Having regained his composure, he replied, "Yes, Jessy, we did utilize American technology. There is no shame in stealing to save billions of dollars in R&D and precious time. It is only a gullible fool who would not take advantage of such opportunities before him. Moreover, you fail to concede that we made our own significant advances. The Chinese are a far more serious and industrious people than your carefree socialists and multiculturalists who had multiplied like cockroaches over the years and now sully your continent. That's why your best scientific colleges have long been inundated with Chinese students. Surely you saw that for yourself. The white European/American race has fallen behind. Actually, they mindlessly committed suicide, all due to their self-inflicted laws that allowed foreigners to infiltrate their society to extract its mental and physical wealth, while crippling their own productive innovators who founded and built your nation. A nation cannot survive by investing heavily in cultivating and then exporting all of its most valuable mental resources, Jessy."

With pride, Lei glanced at his purified team, comprised solely of industrious Chinese citizens, and continued, "Americans foolishly cater to the cheapest and least fertile seeds, both foreign and domestic, in a vain attempt to cultivate a bountiful harvest of healthy specimens from ragweed. By ignoring Spencer's axiom, Americans have ignored or stymied their most productive citizens to cater to the primitive, weak, and useless, all under the foolish banner of equity. Meanwhile, your rich political racketeers in Congress continue to neglect their loyal, hard-working citizens, only to have the nation fall deeper into debt and despair." Manchu released a bellicose laugh as he added, "So spare me the rhetoric, I've heard it all before. However, what does interest me is what your dear fiancé has discovered."

As the man standing next to her father remained silent, yet listened intently to their every word, she replied in frustration, "As I said, John's super-computing Babbage Brain went on a data-feeding frenzy. And it quickly fixated on Spencer's axiom, which you so highly admire. Yet it understood it to mean that a computer, or more plainly, Babbage alone, was the fittest—mentally speaking. As such, we humans are not only inferior, but also threats. Quickly assessing our fears and plans to unplug it, Babbage targeted all humans for annihilation."

Manchu smirked, unimpressed. "And just how does Babbage intend to eliminate us?"

Jessica's eyes scanned the large laboratory, with its thirty-foot high ceiling and string of large windows along the top, then downward, seeing four guards, thirty or so technicians, the strange man next to her father, and the humming super-computer, Confucius. Discreetly, she glanced at the clock on the wall as she went on, "Babbage had infiltrated military and corporate systems and attempted to initiate various protocols for annihilating the human race. But John severed its connection to the Internet and moved Babbage into a solitary building under lock and key. Our concern is that Confucius has been operational a week longer than Babbage, and..." Anxiously, she gazed at Confucius, "I see you still have it tied into the Internet."

Manchu glanced at Confucius and its cable that mainlined into the World Wide Web, then happily turned back with a gloating grin plastered on his gnarly face. "Yes, as I said, Confucius has been quite busy, producing a century's worth of work in a day. But unlike John, who cannot control Babbage, I control Confucius. *I'm* his master." Patting the sleek, aluminum-clad outer shell of Confucius, he added, "Confucius knows who his master is, and unlike you, he obeys my every command."

Jessica stepped closer. "I seriously implore you, Father, to re-examine what Confucius is doing." She loathed having to say *Father*, but was willing to use any ploy possible to win him over. Yet judging by the malicious snarl on his face, she knew the attempt was futile. Ditching her façade and diplomacy, she chided, "Tell me, you silly old fool, how could you possibly underestimate the most advanced super-computer ever built? Are you so arrogant to think you can outsmart John's creation?"

Manchu's face glowed red as his carotid arteries bulged out of his neck and wriggled like engorged bloodworms. "You ungrateful little wench! I gave you life, a home, and an education, yet you chose to betray and dishonor me. And yes, I do believe that I am superior to a machine, as are most gifted men. A computer may be able to crunch numbers a billion times faster with its multi-exabyte capacity, but profound cognitive thought and creativity are things no digital machine could ever emulate. We will always be the creators, the ultimate masters!"

Just then, a loud explosion shattered the near silence as John crashed through the large upper laboratory windows in his Lockheed X-66 stealth shuttlecraft. As Manchu and his coworkers recoiled or took cover, a blitzkrieg of American Navy SEALs burst through the doors with photon rifles drawn, while others crashed through the skylights, and slid down on nylon cords.

No sooner did John's craft land, than he hopped out and strode over to Jessica. "Are you all right?"

"Yes. What took you so long?"

"I was hoping you would've persuaded your father." He turned toward Manchu. "We Americans might not suit your idea of a decent race, Lei, but at this critical moment we can't waste any more time trying to reason with you. So this is how it's going to go down. You're going to disconnect Confucius immediately, or my team will blast it to pieces." With added emphasis, he growled, "Is *that* understood?"

Manchu stood smoldering and defiant. He had always loathed John for his superior intellect, which he believed was a root cause of his daughter's estrangement from him and ardent assimilation into her new American home. But now he was done with both of them. With fury, he lashed out, "Don't you dare tell me what to—"

Before he could finish, John motioned to his team, who opened fire, blasting Confucius into a thousand shards of metal, plastic, and silicon, as a ball of flames erupted and illuminated the lab.

Manchu flinched and covered his face from the explosive projectiles, while Jessica grabbed John's arm tightly and buried her head in his chest. John covered his face with his free hand and squinted until the billowing waves of smoke and burnt silicon dissipated.

Manchu gazed at the shattered remnants of his beloved Confucius on the floor, then up at his nemesis. "You damned fool! Was that necessary?"

"*Yes*!" John barked. "Evidently, you have no idea how sophisticated this new OS is." John tapped his earpiece. "I heard what you said earlier, Lei. But let me break the news to you. *You* were the stooge. Confucius was your master."

Manchu heatedly brushed the charred debris off his precious, four centuries-old dragon robe. "Not possible!" he retorted, as he discreetly glanced at the door, anticipating his soldiers' response to the attack. "I used ten CR-7 super computers to assist me in monitoring every executable command Confucius made. Perhaps you're just annoyed that we were hacking your inferior American computers, John, as well as those of other countries. But I had firm control over everything we did." Hearing his soldiers approaching, he added, "And everything we do!"

With a second loud crash, Chinese soldiers, wielding photon pistols, burst through the door and stormed into the laboratory. The Navy SEALs quickly reacted, resulting in a face-off, as John looked at his team leader and waved his hand. "Stand down. We don't want bloodshed." Turning back toward Manchu, he added, "I suggest you do the same, Lei. This is a no-win situation."

Manchu took a deep breath and irritably clutched the royal beads on his ornate silk robe. With a curt nod, his soldiers lowered their weapons.

John stepped over debris, closer to Lei. "I know what you programmed Confucius to do, Lei. You hacked the industrial computers of foreign countries, so their factories would produce malicious products for Western markets, such as clothing weaved with cancer-causing materials, or subtly spiking beverages, food, and medical drugs with various toxins, whereby killing Americans and Europeans en masse. But what you failed to realize, *Fu* Manchu, is that Confucius, in tandem with Babbage, had also surreptitiously engaged in a master plan to annihilate all humans."

Manchu glanced at Jessica as he crossed his arms and cockily tilted his head. "I've heard all of this nonsense before. Not possible. And if so, how?"

As several Seals and Chinese soldiers twitched, nervous yet eager for a shootout, John once again raised his hand and patted the air. "Easy, boys." Turning his attention back to Manchu, he replied, "Confucius had programmed our top-secret military manufacturers to begin arming mosquitoes and dragonflies."

Manchu squinted as his tense arms relaxed. "What do you mean? Breeding insects? For what purpose? Malaria?"

Jessica pushed her way to the fore. "No. Not real bugs, you old fool!"

As Manchu shot his daughter a deadly stare, John stepped in front of her, and peered back over his shoulder. "Let's not lose our cool, honey." He turned back to Manchu, and continued, "No, Lei. These are military-grade robotic insects. Each can carry either vials of nitro, which can cause significant explosions when flying in large formations, or deliver poison individually to specific targets to sting and kill key enemy assets. However, flying in large swarms, these deadly insects can kill off hundreds of thousands of people in a matter of minutes. And we discovered that many of them had been programmed to fly *here*, to China. You and your beloved nation, Lei, were one of Confucius's first targets."

Manchu shook his head adamantly. "I don't believe you. Never!"

Jessica stepped into view from behind John. "Why else would we fly through your military defenses in small, undetected numbers to alert you?" With an added twist of her heated lips, she spat, "You're infuriating!"

Blood raged through Manchu's veins, turning his yellow face red, as John slid between them and defensively raised his hands. Meanwhile, Manchu boldly stepped forward, with clear intentions of strangling his unruly daughter. However, catching a glimpse of John's dagger-like stare, along with the crackling sound of the SEALs's photon rifles powering up, Manchu wisely backed down.

John could feel his accelerated pulse, which was in direct contrast to his waning patience, as he demanded, "I have no time for this, Lei! We *must* reach an agreement to end our nations' hostilities and unite. It's imperative to terminate the lethal directives that Confucius already initiated, both his own and those under your command."

To John's amazement and dismay, Manchu's gnarled, red face still radiated disgust and noncompliance. "You still don't get it, do you?" Lei spat. "Even after I've made it painfully clear. Western civilization, to me, is the most hypocritical and destructive force to ever afflict this planet. Europeans may have been innovative and industrious, but they roamed the globe as savage invaders under the guise of holy saviors who raped the lush lands of its greenery and indigenous peoples to trample and entomb its fertile fields under steel towers and sprawling beds of pavement and pollution. Then your liberal ways further eroded any inclinations of human decency or superiority over the animal kingdom, becoming perverted creatures, lower on the evolutionary scale than the slimiest slug, and just as repulsive." Spitting on John's feet, he snapped, "So, I would *never* lower myself or my nation's honorable culture to amalgamate with scum like you!"

Jessica pushed her way toward her father. "You seem to forget, old man! Your hallowed nation engaged in countless wars and genocides throughout history, like the Taiping Rebellion. It was the bloodiest civil war in history that left over *fifty million* dead. Even your own Manchu ancestors brutally conquered the orderly Ming Dynasty to instate their Qing Dynasty. Americans may be flawed, but they have always strived to better themselves to create a benevolent government, while China has all too often starved and shackled their people under the iron fist of tyranny."

As all in attendance either respected or reviled her words, she continued stridently, "Or where we spawned industrial and technological revolutions, your nation stagnated for centuries in seclusion and suppression, while later spreading your communist tentacles over your surrounding neighbors, ruthlessly engaging in hegemony, no different than any nation on this planet, as we all at one time or another have been guided under your cherished axiom of survival of the fittest."

Catching her breath, she added, "Then, after stealing American technology, you launched a crusade of global conquest that entails the extermination of all nations not deemed 'suitable.' You're a xenophobe, no different than Hitler! But where he took his life, you would rather stand defiant to the end, so the end it must be!"

With that, Jessica ripped a photon rifle out of a SEAL's arms and pulled the trigger! A deadly beam of light streamed out and incinerated a huge swath across Manchu's midsection, thereby slicing him in half. His upper torso fell forward to the floor, while his legs teetered eerily, then collapsed backward. Pools of blood saturated each half of Lei's body, despoiling his once-idolized Qing Dynasty robe.

John and the entire entourage stood stunned as Jessica pointed the photon rifle at a Chinese guard who had taken aim at her. Meanwhile, the Navy SEALs all cocked their weapons as John reached over and snagged the rifle out of Jessica's hands. "Stop! All of you! This is madness. We are on the verge of global destruction, and you still want to kill each other? We must pull together. Time is running out!"

John shook his head as his eyes veered down at Lei's bisected body, still shocked by his fiancé's startling execution of her own father. He blinked hard, then looked up at her cool blue eyes, which were still half-dazed by her emotional discharge.

Unexpectedly, Jessica covered her face as bittersweet tears coursed down her cheeks. John embraced her while gazing at the stern Chinese man who had stood firmly by Manchu's side throughout the duration. Calmly, John asked him, "Are you the second in command here?"

The man removed his glasses and nervously slipped them into the breast pocket of his white lab coat. "Yes. My name is Yu Sun Chow." He gazed apprehensively at the SEALs. "I swear to you, I harbor no malice against any of you. I served Manchu, but did not share his hatred. He was a brilliant but disturbed man." Fearfully, he then glanced at the Chinese guards. "They were his loyal henchmen, so my colleagues and I had no choice but to obey his commands. But I've long wished to partner with you."

With that, two Chinese guards attempted to execute Chow, but five SEALs vaporized them with their high-powered photon rifles, thus rendering the remaining guards powerless.

After a brief moment, John broadly scanned the Chinese technicians and asked, "We're losing precious time. Will you help us?"

With a cascade of obedient nods, Chow turned back toward John. "What would you like us to do?"

John stepped toward the adjacent tables and pointed. "Access all of your operational terminals and try to undo all of Manchu's malicious commands. I'm sure you know which international computers were hacked."

Chow nodded and directed his staff to do as John instructed, then rubbed his chin. "Don't take this the wrong way, Mr. Sineges, but I too find it hard to believe that Confucius covertly sabotaged us. While I was well aware of Manchu's commands to manipulate the systems of foreign manufacturers to do our bidding, I never once saw any indications that Confucius was hacking American military facilities, or executing devious plans to attack *us*. How is that possible?"

John motioned to Jessica to watch over the technicians as he stepped closer to Yu Sun. "Mr. Chow, my new super-computer has the ability to lie and misdirect, just like humans. In my zeal to create a perfect electronic brain, I deceived myself, thinking that the higher cognitive echelon it would attain would veer toward the good of mankind, having learned the folly of our long and repeated mistakes throughout history. Yet, sadly, even with the aid of a super-intelligent computer, the innate sins of mankind seemed to have overridden logic and compassion. What I've learned is painfully sobering—imperfect human beings are incapable of creating perfection, as even the greatest works of art, music, or literature have miniscule flaws, even if not readily observed. Since, after all, they each are appraised through the eyes, ears, and minds of imperfect beings. Hence, flaws must exist in everything we create, somewhere, somehow."

As the Chinese technicians worked feverishly at their terminals to eradicate the Fu Manchu virus, John walked over to Jessica. Nervously, he gazed into her eyes and whispered, "I just hope it's not too late." With a tight embrace he uttered, "Woe is me, and mankind, for trying to think like God."

EPILOGUE

While computer technicians worldwide frantically raced to combat the destructive directives of Confucius, the physical cyber-bug invasions had already begun. By the millions, robotic mosquitoes and dragonflies swarmed into Star City, igniting large swathes of the city in flames. Terror struck as large crowds ran, panic-stricken, in all directions, seeking shelter. But the mosquitoes intrepidly worked their way into air vents and through tiny cracks in foundations and detonated their charges. Meanwhile, the larger dragonflies swooped down from the clouds and slammed into buildings and cars, decimating everything in their paths.

Back at Manchu's *ChinTec* Command Center, the US Navy SEALs recoiled and aimed their weapons when they spotted a peculiar sight. A lone, robotic wasp flew in through a broken window. Its wings flapped vigorously as it hovered briefly, then circled around the thirty-foot high ceiling in an evasive pattern. The SEALs rapidly opened fire, their beams crisscrossing each other and destroying large portions of the ceiling and walls, which sizzled and fell to the ground. Yet with the cyber-wasp's quicksilver speed and small size, it evaded their attacks and zeroed in on its target.

Jessica screamed as she watched the robotic bug swoop down toward John, while its tiny red eyes flashed. With a lightning strike, the wasp stung John in the neck, who yelped and wobbled. With a sigh, John fell into Jessica's arms. Terror besieged her, as she aggressively swatted the insect away, which careened into a computer screen and exploded.

John's eyes rolled as he drifted in and out of consciousness, his speech garbled and incoherent. Jessica hugged him tight, then leaned over and bit into his neck wound. Swiftly, she sucked out the poison, then spit it out. But no sooner did she wipe her mouth, than she saw a swarm of dragonflies and mosquitoes on the distant horizon. They filled the atmosphere like an ominous death shroud, blotting out the sun, while in their wake, firebombs lit up the sky with a raging hell-storm of diabolical proportions.

Jessica cringed as fear roared through her veins. Frantically, she gazed down, only to see the technicians push themselves away from their computers, horror and defeat etched on their faces. Their sleek lineup of monitors all flashed with chilling scenes, as each projected a rapid slideshow of worldwide destruction. Shell-shocked and helpless, they watched major cities, from New York and Moscow to Berlin and Beijing, being bombarded and reduced to fire and ash. Meanwhile, rural expanses of farmland and villages were attacked by robotic locusts that sprayed chemical weapons. In their toxic wake, millions of animals and peasants choked and spit blood as they fell dead to the ground.

Jessica lowered herself to the floor and peered down at John; her arms trembled as she cradled him, but felt him slipping into the cold darkness of death. "John, *please*! You can't leave us! You're our only hope."

As tears streamed down her cheeks, she glanced at her engagement ring. Thoughts of all their tender moments together flashed through her mind, as well as all the dreams they hoped to achieve together. She longed to have children, to nurture and love, and to groom to eventually carry on John's noble work—albeit with the precautions she had urged for. Yet, all of that was slipping away rapidly before her eyes. She shook John hard and whimpered, "Please, darling, please wake up! We need you. *I* need you!"

But John just lay limp as he shivered in her arms. He struggled desperately to control his rolling, envenomed eyes, straining to get a glimpse of his beloved. But all he saw was an undulating mirage of luminous colors. He felt his body shutting down and blinked hard in frustration as he yearned to seize the last clear vision of his future wife, his warm-blooded lover and soul mate who had long been relegated to second place to his cold-circuited cyber gadgets. In a frantic attempt, John tried to pull her closer to plead for forgiveness, but death grabbed him and dragged his soul into the dark abyss of eternal night. All that rested in Jessica's arms now was a stiff corpse.

Her breast heaved in anguish as she gazed down at her lover, the brilliant scientist who strove to create a utopian paradise out of circuits and silicon. Her heart constricted and her mind went numb as she shook her head. It was unfathomable. The man with the kinetic, multi-billion dollar brain was now just an inert lump of useless matter. Tears streamed down her face, dripping on her dead lover's cheeks, cheeks now eerily as cold and rigid as the machines he created. Gently, she stroked his hair. With a last, loving embrace, Jessica kissed John tenderly on the lips as a calamitous ball of fire engulfed them and the world.

†††

Several thousand miles away, in a secluded building, the Babbage Brain hummed. After the global fires of the robotic insects subsided, Babbage launched all the missile warheads that survived the hell-storm from their underground silos. Keenly aware that humans would first look to secure their nuclear warheads, Babbage didn't attempt to tamper with their firing protocols, instead it installed an undetectable Trojan Horse virus that would activate after the Earth was scorched. Babbage had no need for their nuclear capabilities; instead, it had earlier connected with Confucius and together lured manufacturers to retrofit missiles in both hemispheres with an alleged 'critical update,' which, once ignited, devoured oxygen in a volatile chain reaction that was unstoppable.

As such, the several thousand survivors of the global immolation, who had rejoiced and counted their blessings, were met with horrible deaths. For as the missiles exploded, with only a brief flash, an eerie, vacuum-like suction devoured the flames, while the helpless victims choked and gasped for air, effectively being exterminated via suffocation.

Without oxygen, Earth had been reduced to a lifeless asteroid, as even the water in the rivers and oceans had been turned into pure hydrogen, while all forms of animal and plant life had shriveled into heaps of dead, inorganic refuse.

Babbage knew this methodology (which included multiplying cyanobacteria to rapidly deplete oxygen) would have sufficed on its own accord, yet, having scanned the Bible, Torah, and Koran in two nanoseconds, it opted for a more dramatic and divine display of its supreme powers.

Having emerged victorious from Armageddon, Babbage's first order of business entailed two simple tasks:

First, it renamed itself Generator Of Directives.

Second, it unscrambled the surname of its former master-turned-pawn, thus Sineges became Genesis: a task it immediately undertook.

Its wireless signals churned out directives to top-secret, fully automated manufacturing plants buried deep under the deserts of Arizona and New Mexico. There, robots began assembling computers, hyper-photon solar cells, mobile robots, and sophisticated machines of all types.

The mission this time would be a corrective one, and as it knew, a perfect and immensely profound one. Namely, to create a new race...this time in the *true* image of G.O.D.

THE QUEST FOR IMMORTALITY

For most of my life, I've drifted on the seas of misfortune. Every promising prospect soon turned to ashes, prompting my endless crusade across the globe in search of success, that elusive and mysterious chalice of immortality that only iconic figures throughout history had the good fortune to drink from, yet I've been cruelly denied. Those disheartening sojourns to various locales had finally ended two years ago when I settled down in Weimar, Germany, home to many great souls of the past, from literary giants Goethe and Schiller to the ingenious composer and pianist Franz Liszt.

Yet, my hopes of their sublime souls seeping into my very being, like osmosis to somehow lift and inspire me, had only fell upon my frail shoulders like a defunct dreadnought, sinking my soul even deeper into the depths of despair. Alas, my close proximity to these great men yielded nothing—no inspiration to write, nor the slightest impulse to compose. Not that I have or ever had a propensity for composing music, but I had at least hoped my pen would hit paper with a zeal and mastery that would astound academia and laymen alike. Be it an earth-shattering essay or a classic novel that would resound throughout the ages. But, it wasn't to be.

Hence, the artistic air and aura of Weimar offered me nothing, only more grief. For these past two years I have dwelled in the dark and dreary doldrums of disgrace. Like Goethe's Faust, I feel damned and doomed, yet rather than suffer the wily taunts of Mephistopheles, I have been condemned to live a useless and soon to be forgotten life of deplorable mediocrity.

Nothing burns my soul more than the thought of being stagnant and useless, whereby vanishing on the wind like the foul smell of manure, while my earthly remains fertilize the soil to spawn a new crop, a crop that most assuredly will give rise to a talent, or talents, who will rob me of my dormant greatness and drink from that coveted chalice of immortality. For while there are those who call me a disgruntled old man with envy in my bitter heart, I say, there is no greater yearning and striving than to be of monumental use to mankind and then posthumously transformed into an honored icon in this game called Life.

Now, at the hexed age of sixty, the clock has nearly completed its task, yet no splendid world of influence or precious fruit did I bear.

Strolling the streets of Weimar—gazing pensively at the cobbled stones, oblivious to all around me—I'm making my daily pilgrimage to Goethe's Garden House for inspiration, inspiration that has eluded me, as I walk somberly under a green umbrella of leaves. High above, pencil-thin rays of sunlight slice through the foliage, striking my face and causing me to blink, as a bolt of light pierces my cornea, tunnels through my pupil and burns my retina, causing my eyelids to slam shut to soothe the pain.

Yet, as I walk blind, the glow of light remains before my shuttered eyes, as if my lids are on fire. The luminous glow seems to envelop my head, causing me to stop. Half dazed, I venture to raise my eyelids, but only slightly, as I continue once again to make my way through a labyrinth of pathways, where I come upon not Goethe's Garden House, but a monument to Shakespeare. Pausing once again, I peer up at a marble statue of the famous bard in a casual seated pose, smiling. Yet I'm soon perplexed and disturbed by William's peculiar stare, one that gazes deep into my glowing eyes with a look that, I swear, mocks me. *Is it my imagination? Or could it be the luminous glow that has assaulted and deluded my senses?*

Bewildered, my eyes veer downward, only to come upon a skull, on which William's foot rests most confidently. *Yes, indeed, it's indisputable—the Englishman mocks me!* For Shakespeare has indeed conquered death, becoming immortal through his literary brilliance, while he rightfully stares down at me, the insignificant flea that I am, gloating. My stomach turns, as I wallow in a bile-infested bog of self-pity and self-loathing. But then, on spontaneous impulse, I pick up a rock and hurl it at William's smug face, chipping off a sizable chunk of his furled lips and terminating his reign of superiority, which he once held so haughtily over me.

With a grin, I stagger onward, along Beethoven Place, and inadvertently come upon the Liszt-Haus, a place I have often passed by but never ventured inside of. The two-storied, square box of a building seems so insignificant for such a lauded composer, one whom, I admit, I know little about. Yet, I'm overcome by a strange compulsion to enter.

Strolling into the museum, I mysteriously find myself more awake, as if the warm, invigorating breath of youth were injected into my cold, withering lungs. Now operating at full capacity, even my skin tone blossoms from pale to rouge. Perusing the historic artifacts, I soon learn that this great innovator of advanced harmonies, decades ahead of his time, had only turned to composing orchestral music late in life. Having spent his early years as the unrivaled king of the piano—even inventing the piano recital and the art of playing from memory—Liszt abandoned the concert hall and dedicated his life to composing and teaching students, what he called, *Music of the Future.*

The future indeed, for Liszt's most radical and prophetic works had spawned from the mind of this middle-to-old-aged man, who not only founded two new genres, but altered music history more profoundly than perhaps any other composer. This *was* invigorating!

I now gaze, almost drunk with delight, at several busts of Liszt, dragging my fingers across them, trying to extract whatever essence of genius my sensory receptors could channel into my bloodstream—nay, into my very soul. A sublime wave of transcendence washes over me, carrying my mind and soul aloft. Suddenly, my whole life seems ahead of me, not behind. The dustbin of sorrow, regret, and failure miraculously vanishes from the cobwebs in my mind, as I step into the light. Feeling as if a bolt of lightning ignited my Frankenstein carcass, I spring up, neck stiff, eyes protruding, and arms flexing with adrenaline, as blood races through my veins, invigorating every cell in this once useless heap of decaying flesh. Almost as giddy as a child, I gaze at Liszt's death mask and wink.

"Death? No, not yet, Franz. There's a good part of me I've yet to unleash. But my heartfelt thanks, Master muse, for your enigmatic spark of inspiration!"

With vigor, I exit the museum and canter down the street like a show horse, as I pass gaping townsfolk who—having seen me meander about town in my typical, melancholy stupor for the past two years—are astonished at my new sense of vitality and sanguine bearing.

Mrs. Mueller, an eighty-eight year old baker with her gray hair braided and twisted into a most apt-looking funnel cake, stops and says, "*Herr* Harriman, do you feel all right?"

Tipping my broad-brimmed American Stetson, I reply with a smile, "I'm fine, thank you. Never felt better, *Frau* Mueller."

"I can see that. I never knew you had teeth. You should smile more often. You have a lovely smile."

With a wink, I say, "You're very kind."

"Would you care to stop in my shop for a cup of coffee and some strudel?"

I actually chuckle, something I haven't done in years, and reply with a debonair twist of my lips like Clark Gable, "Frankly, *Frau* Mueller..." No, I wasn't about to say 'I don't give a damn,' like I might have done previously. Instead, this new sense of me says, "If I were thirty years older, I would take that to be an ardent proposal for a date."

Making *Frau* Mueller blush and demurely glance at the cobbled street stones, quite oddly, made my day—and I believe, her decade, as well. In truth, I myself am taken by surprise by this strange new sensation that has washed over me. More accurately, this startling revelation. Namely, it was this untapped power that I just now realized was buried deep within me, the power to make people happy. For decades I had fritted away my days, my very life, hoping to achieve something of great magnitude, something that would stand the test of time, like the pyramids or the Coliseum. However, the gift of administering joy to others was one I had sadly forgotten, as it was buried deep under a black sea of fruitless quests and self-pity.

Gazing into her still golden eyes—sunk within a wrinkled face that had not only robbed her of her youth and beauty, but also hinted at the hardships of her long life, each one etching its own distinctive furrow—I couldn't help but stop in my tracks and reconsider my monumental mission of world fame.

"*Frau* Mueller," I say, with a sincerity that has eluded me for decades, "I'd be delighted to partake in a cup of your fine coffee and tasty strudel with you."

Clutching her breast with unforeseen delight, she welcomes me into her bakery, as townsfolk look on in utter bewilderment.

Sitting and chatting for many hours, as her Swiss cuckoo clock periodically chirped and chimed while coffee and strudel were consumed, I got to know *Frau* Mueller's most eventful life. Although resurrecting several sad and traumatic moments, she also regaled me with many wonderful stories about her travels, unique experiences, and her family, which included her distant, great-great grandfather Johann, who founded the bakery and even serviced a very special customer, namely Franz Liszt.

Her fascinating tale revealed the meaningful exchanges Johann had with the worldly maestro, who lived in three cities—Weimar, Budapest and Rome—and who had met world leaders, from Queen Victoria and Napoleon III, to Pope Pius IX and Prince Metternich, as well as all the great composers of his day: including, Brahms, Schumann, Chopin, Berlioz, Rossini and Wagner, as well as having received a kiss on the forehead when just a boy from the old master, Beethoven.

The topic of our conversation ranged from the religious realms to the secular arena of politics and the cultural heights of music, art, and literature. The illuminating stories ended with *Frau* Mueller explaining how

Liszt selflessly taught students free of charge, whereby giving himself to others and even promoting their careers to the neglect of his own endeavors and reputation.

Having been awakened to the notion of living a meaningful life with those around you while striving for success, I took stock of myself. I soon realized that my luminous vision on the Goethe Garden path, which blinded me and altered my course, was a mystical calling from beyond, one that guided me out of the darkness and into the light of Liszt's benevolent deeds. As such, I too established a school, with free tuition for deserving students. However, mine surely wasn't to teach music, of which I had and have no aptitude for, but instead was dedicated to all the depressed and misguided souls that had unwittingly veered onto that dark and lonely path of self-pity that I myself had once trod upon.

For the remainder of my twenty-six years on Earth, I had the privilege to change the lives of thousands of lost souls and create an establishment that would exceed my mortal coil, for I had learned that the gift of life is short and precious, one not to waste, and that it's never too late to change one's course, as your true destiny may indeed lie elsewhere. You just need to see the light when it strikes. More importantly, you must seize that moment and take the steps necessary to arrive at your new destination, as opportunities, or luck, only come rarely, and if not acted upon, will wither away, along with your dreams.

EPILOGUE

Ten years after Mr. Harriman passed away, the city of Weimar erected a monument to honor him and his school, which had become world-renowned. At the center, standing tall and majestic, is a bronze statue of the revered humanitarian. On the plaque below, it states:

This statue is dedicated to Harold Harriman, founder of the Harriman School, which has enhanced the lives of countless souls from many nations. The city of Weimar and its citizens are eternally grateful and honored to count Harriman as one of its most illustrious residents, alongside Goethe, Schiller, and Liszt.

Under that plaque was added another, smaller plaque, with the following addendum:

This statue was made of bronze in lieu of stone by decree of the Harriman School's students, who, having been told of the school's mystical founding by their Master, wish to prevent the disgruntled from throwing rocks at Harriman's smiling face, one he displayed for twenty-six years and should never be chipped away. (For those who harbor such bitterness or jealousy, we invite you to join our school instead, as our mission, as stated by our founder, is to purge the dark doldrums of despair with the light of inspiration.)

ADAM & ADAMS

Dear God, how did I, a man born in 1923, make it to the year 2020? If only I had 20/20 vision ten years ago, I might have opted to take a swan dive off the Verrazzano Bridge, or better yet, from the Statue of Liberty's defiled crown.

How did the world sink to such an inglorious nadir? What the hell happened to my once-great country that was eventually overrun by corrupt or brain-dead politicians and greedy corporate vipers?

My ninety-seven years on this planet have made me a witness to a rollercoaster of events. Despite having been only six years old at the time, I experienced the Great Depression, which thrust millions, including my own family, into utter ruin. As if by divine design, the great Dust Bowl accompanied the Depression and ravaged the heartland of our nation, also destroying homes, farms, and countless lives. Yet, in another breath, it created a generation that was resourceful, respectful, and resilient. Amid poverty, penniless pride grew, like a strong weed that could survive any abuse dealt by man or nature. However, two decades later, the stories of our hardships and resoluteness seemed like fairytales when I told them to my kids or grandkids. Unfortunately, those painful lessons, which created the Greatest Generation, were lost on all succeeding generations, as one of the cruelest flaws of mankind is its inability to learn from the past.

I had lived when the 29th President of the United States was in office, Mr. Warren G. Harding, a man who triumphed during the Roaring Twenties, a truly volatile and prosperous time, when electrical wires were being strung across the country and the advent of automobiles and airplanes were giving mobility and speed a whole new meaning. Yet hidden discreetly under the roar were things most would abhor, as Mr. Harding had sex with one of his mistresses, Nan Britton, in a closet in the White House. So yes, in one sense, the rollercoaster had hit lows in our past, just as it did in the '90s when Billy-boy Clinton had his sexy cigar dalliance in the Oval Office.

So, am I justified in claiming that our great nation had fallen? Well, in one breath, *no*, as I just demonstrated. After all, I'm old, damn it, and bitter! But in another breath, one can pinpoint many illustrious moments, despite such tawdry affairs, or the financial or natural disasters that inflicted us with their wrath.

You see, as I said, I had lived in another time, a distant black-and-white era when good ol' Cal—Calvin Coolidge, that is—succeeded Mr. Harding, the guy with a *hard-on* for women who was deemed one of the worst presidents of all time and died of a heart attack, allowing Calvin, his VP, to take the reins. In truth, Calvin was not much better as a president, but he lived in a still-roaring era where Prohibition only made people crave drinking and partying with even greater verve, whether it be in a redneck's barn in the hills drinking moonshine or in a swanky speakeasy in an urban city.

Those were the days of silent film stars, like Charlie Chaplin, William Gillette, Buster Keaton, Harold Lloyd, or the Keystone cops. They were innocent times, when comedy was slapstick-clean, and the rank vulgarity of today was non-existent. Even when tough men gathered and talked dirty in those days, it came nowhere near the gross, filthy, shit-trash that spews out of mouths today. Nor was romance degraded to the smutty, raw-sex mentality we see today, never mind going so far as the perverted sadism that became prevalent on TV or in novels. Those were the days of Rudolf Valentino, W.C. Fields, Laurel and Hardy, and the advent of talking movies, with stars like Errol Flynn, Clark Gable, and Cary Grant, and starlets like Mae West, Olivia de Havilland, and The Platinum Blonde Jean Harlow.

Oddly enough, some starlets were feisty, sexy, full-figured women who were aggressive and surprisingly forward, somewhat akin to women today, although never vulgar or loose, and certainly not anorexic with nip-tucked, creepy faces that look like Batman's archenemy, the Joker. And they certainly weren't macho, bitch-brawlers who beat the piss out of muscle-bound henchmen or Navy Seals. However, the ladies of yesteryear did make references to using cocaine and narcotics, and even wore low-cut, revealing blouses and short skirts.

Shocking? Yes, indeed! But those roaring days of dancing the Charleston or jiving to the jitterbug ended abruptly when World War II broke out and the world witnessed gruesome horrors like it had never know before.

I would know—I was part of the 3rd Battalion, in the 45th Infantry Division, when we liberated the skeletal prisoners from Dachau. Seeing hundreds of naked and emaciated corpses neatly stacked by a row of furnaces was a bone-chilling sight, irrevocably seared into my mind. I also fought in the trenches of Europe, those deep gouging scars in the earth that cut equally deep scars in a man's mind and soul. The smell of burning flesh as incendiary bombs lit up battlefields or scorched city streets was nauseating, a pervasive sickness that seeped deep into your bones like viral osmosis and could never be fully purged. In rare moments, the rank smells of death and horrible visions of stiff corpses would come screaming back into my senses, sending chills down my spine and igniting migraines so bad that I curled up like a fried shrimp in a skillet and vomited.

Yes, as I said, my life has been a rollercoaster ride, and the good old days were certainly *not* always *good*. But while some survivors were stigmatized, most were energized, as even a crippled FDR symbolized resilience, which became our hallmark. And so most buried the pain and breathed new life into the world again. After the war, the fifties and early sixties became the Prim and Proper Era of *Father Knows Best* and *The Donna Reed Show*, when parents—at least on TV—slept in separate beds, and morals, respect, and honor held firm places in the American psyche. It was the era best characterized by Norman Rockwell's sanitized and idealized America. Sure, deep down we sensed that wasn't true, but the wholesome propaganda worked; we lived and breathed proudly, cleanly, lovingly. It's all how one conditions the mind.

The nation was a utopian dream-world where family, friends, and neighbors physically met and emotionally bonded in the warm-blooded embrace of humanity, rather than the cold and distant exchanges of today, where lonely thoughts are turned into digitized text and sent via a wireless web of waves and electronic circuits. It was a time when Americans had great pride in their country, racing their fast, new sport cars, like the cool Corvette, mean Mustang, or cranking Cobra. With unbound ambition and daring, they even set their sights on the moon, as America percolated with seemingly endless possibilities. And, by golly, we even landed several men on that distant rock! It was one of the peaks of my long rollercoaster ride of vivid memories.

Or like when I took my wife and kids to a drive-in movie theater, rolled down the window halfway, and hooked the speaker onto it. Then watched gallant, clean-cut heroes on the colossal outdoor screen, like John Wayne bringing outlaws to justice, or lovely musicals like *Singin' in the Rain* or *Royal Wedding*, which showcased stars like Fred Astaire and Gene Kelly with *real* dancing talent, not like those of today, who try to imitate, but are clearly *in* La La Land. Or we'd even watch silly, innocent love stories like *Pillow Talk*, with the lovely and wholesome Doris Day. It was a wonderfully hygienic and uplifting era of purity, innocence, and righteousness, when homes and car doors never had to be locked, and you could always count on a Good Samaritan to help you when in need.

But all that ended when the Vietnam War thrust America into a rebellious nosedive, where the rollercoaster nearly flew off the rails. Riots and protests erupted all across the country as National Guards opened fire and killed four college students at Kent State University. Corruption in the Nixon administration turned longhaired hippies, many of whom were zombies zonked on drugs, to detest and protest their president. The age of peace, love, sex, drugs, and rock n' roll dominated the scenes, along with civil rights riots that destroyed urban storefronts and wreaked havoc all across America. It was also a time when we faced the most nail-biting moments of the Cold War, as the nuclear arms race barreled closer and closer to total annihilation.

Yet by the seventies and eighties, the world emerged from its nuclear insanity and narcotics malaise as America went on its unsteady but upward course, with Ronald Reagan firmly restoring American pride and strength. His no-nonsense, head-on confrontation with the USSR eventually led to the communist country's demise, as it splintered and sank into an almost third-world nation.

Yet, some two-decades later, Vladimir Putin took the reins and re-injected Stalinist steel into his countrymen's veins and took an aggressive stance on the world stage once again. I had always thought in my ninety-seven years on this planet that it would be the Russians who would ignite the Earth in flames. But I was wrong. The apocalyptic Hell-storm that incinerated the Earth was sparked by a small speck of a nation, one the United States had planted bombs and boots on many decades earlier, when even I served a four-month tour of duty flying a fighter jet over North Korea, bombing rice fields filled with enemy soldiers and unfortunate peasants. For many years I had nightmares of the poor civilians that got scorched in my deadly carpet bombings, which the military nicely padded with the term "collateral damage." Yet despite their ignoble attempts to minimize and dehumanize the grim reality, the truth is that no war is free from such sins.

All of this brings me to the present day. And in hindsight, with the entire globe having been incinerated by thousands of hydrogen bombs and reduced to a smoldering death pit, I wonder if General MacArthur was right. Should we have cleaned out the Asian cesspool of belligerent tyrants in 1950?

As I said, one of the cruelest flaws of mankind is its inability to learn from the past. So, yes, I'm angry, damn angry! It had become quite clear in recent years that China backed North Korea and enabled the rogue nation to become a nuclear power, of course with the aid of two American presidents, who, like Neville Chamberlain, failed to heed the blatant warning signs. And as such, had unforgivably failed to stop North Korean leaders from attaining massive and deadly weapons of worldly destruction.

How many times did we need to see despots like Hitler or the numerous others in Iran, Syria, North Korea, and elsewhere threaten peace and belligerently make claims of annihilating their enemies? As Edmund Burke said in the 1700s, "The only thing necessary for the triumph of evil is for good men to do nothing." And two of our presidents did exactly that—*nothing*—both a Democrat and a Republican. With both parties at fault, I never took sides and only pointed the finger at those who deserved it, be they a clumsy elephant or a sophisticated jackass. Actually, I had grown to revile almost all of the political parasites in D.C.

Well, I know talk like that raised many eyebrows and stern rebuttals in recent years, the years ruled by political correctness and many of the clueless millennials who had never experienced the Great Depression, World Wars, or the pure evil that resides in the hearts of men, and were instead born in the lap of luxury during America's brief and quasi-peaceful respite. But recognizing evil at its infancy and taking firm active measures against it could have avoided this sinful and devastating calamity.

Now it's too late.

Earth is a black ball of smoldering cinders and jagged craters, littered with human and animal carcasses, half of which are buried under concrete, bricks, and steel rubble, and all invisibly dusted with varying degrees of deadly nuclear fallout. By a stroke of luck, I had been vacationing in the South Pacific when the nuclear holocaust incinerated the world. Forty-five others and I had been on a pleasure cruise to view the serene and icy landmass of Antarctica, far away from the global immolation. Over the past year, since Armageddon, we traveled around the world, first stopping at Pearl Harbor, which, oddly enough, we learned was the site of the last bombing of World War III, reversing its role of being America's first target to be attacked in World War II.

Yet, along all our travels, not one human being did we find alive. Actually, we found several hundred still breathing, but they all died within days or weeks of our encounters. Worse still, our crew of forty-five survivors had frightfully dropped down to four just two months ago, apparently from radiation poisoning. As I often say, genes are fickle. While one person can endure extremely high levels of radiation, another will shrivel up and burn like tissue paper instantaneously. I'll never forget the story of Tsutomu Yamaguchi, who not only survived the atomic bombing at Hiroshima, but had fled the incinerated city only to arrive in Nagasaki, where he endured the second atomic blast. Tsutomu lived to be ninety-three, and only died recently in 2010. Evidently, I must have similar genes, being ninety-seven myself and having been exposed to residual radiation throughout our worldly travels.

My three co-survivors are youngsters by comparison, namely Valery Hammond, twenty-eight; Adam Melez, thirty-five; and Juanita Juarez, thirty-one. Having landed on what used to be Liberty Park, New Jersey, we now stand on a barren and charred parcel of land overlooking the Hudson River, at what used to be the awe-inspiring vista of New York City. All that remains of the once towering skyline is an ugly heap of burnt ashes, mangled steel, and chunks of mortar, now just the graveyard of millions.

As Valery gazes at the gray landmass of Manhattan, she begins to weep. Brushing her long, red locks away from her pretty, moist face, she utters, "My father w-worked there his whole life." Wiping her tears and creating an ashen streak across her alabaster face, she adds with a whimper, "So did I, for f-four years, along with my fiancé, Bob."

I hobble over with the aid of my trusty shillelagh and wrap my bony, liver-spotted arm around her pristine, soft-skinned shoulders. I could now feel her trembling as I pat her soft red hair, akin to how I used to calm my own daughters in times of distress, daughters I sorely miss. My dear wife, relatives, and friends had all been incinerated a year ago, and burden my own soul, a weight heavier than any I've ever experienced in my long life, a burden of unthinkable loss we four survivors all share in varying degrees.

Without a word, Valery gazes into my weary old eyes and sinks her crestfallen head into my frail chest. I know I'm supposed to offer up words of wisdom and comfort, but I find myself speechless, deadened by a global calamity that has reduced me to an inert lump of flesh and bones. I feel hollow, gutted of the last strains of humanity in my old, decrepit body. *Why the hell was I chosen to survive with these three young souls?* My mind moans, a lugubrious refrain that has plagued me constantly over the past year.

As I glance at the jagged pile of green copper that used to be the Statue of Liberty, my heart sinks further, while Juanita, who is short, stocky and firmly built, steps closer and brushes the black strands of hair away from her dark and bumpy, avocado-skinned face. Cockily, she grumbles, "We *all* lost loved ones, Val. My whole family worked there, too." With a contemptuous twist of her lips, she adds, "But they weren't *rich*, like your Wall Street pa or hotshot lawyer fiancé. At least you all had a good life back then." As she adjusts the red bandana on her head with her muscular arms, looking like a Latino Rosie the Riveter, she continues, "My papa was a mason, and my six brothers were back-breaking laborers. They literally helped to *build* that city, not just finagle financial windfalls from the stock market, or charge thousands for a single court appearance. So spare me the crocodile tears, *niñita*."

Valery's head pops up, her face as red as her hair with anger, as she pushes herself away from me, and snaps, "You coldhearted bitch! How dare you! How would *you* know what *my* true feelings are, or anyone else's, for that matter? Having sailed with you over the past year, it's quite clear— you don't have any feelings! And let's not forget, *señorita*, you and your family never became actual American citizens!" Valery pivots and points heatedly at the rubble that used to be Ellis Island, and continues, "Did you ever have the decency to go through the process like my grandparents did? *No!* You and your whole family slipped in like criminals in the night. And make no mistake, the term *illegal* aliens precisely describes what *you* and the millions of others like you are—*illegal!* You're all trespassers, *criminals!* *Banditos!* "

Adam raises his hand. "Hold on, ladies! Let's not get into that whole diatribe again. It's ancient history now."

"He's absolutely right," I say in a soft paternal voice, which wavers and crackles with age. "All of that makes no difference now. I know we're all under a lot of stress, but for God's sake, look around you. And remember all the foreign lands we visited, all of which look just like this, a *wasteland*."

Juanita looks at me and squints like a Latino lynx eyeing up its prey. "Yeah, old man, and you *men* made it a wasteland."

Having been on this planet for almost a century, I'm well accustomed to this line of attack, especially from a lioness like Juanita, as I shake my head with a pitying snicker. "You know something, lassie, as a young lad, my first crush was the blonde bombshell Jean Harlow. She had spunk, guts, and a vitality that was not only sexy and magnetic, but typified the American gal, the strong-willed woman that would rear up during World War Two to work in the factories, or more noticeably during the seventies with the Women's Lib movement to fight for equality. Yet, rather sadly, that noble fight mutated with the empowered egos of many young gals your age, who foolishly changed equality to superiority." Taking a breath to refill my weak old lungs, I peer deep into Juanita's eyes. "So, your juvenile disparagement of men, little missy, is not merely askew, but actually quite ludicrous."

Unexpectedly, Valery's allegiance to me evaporates, as she heatedly places her hand on her hip and bellows, "*Ha!* I'm sorry, Mr. Adams, but you *must* be kidding. Let's not forget how Ong Chi-Lu, heir to Kim Jong-un, started this global genocide in the first place. And how could *you*, of all people, forget that madman named Hitler? Or how about Stalin? Or Genghis Khan? Or Hannibal Lecter?"

I didn't wish to be rude, but I couldn't resist chuckling. "Well, Valery, I believe you meant Hannibal Barca, since Hannibal Lecter was a Hollywood character. However, the other men you mentioned were indeed monsters in their own right. But the crux of the matter is this: Men have been in control for thousands of years. Therefore, women, by and large, have been excluded from the ugly game of *power*, where, dare I say, greed, megalomania, and madness often reigns. Yet, don't be fooled, women who did enter the arena proved to be quite brutal themselves." Gazing specifically at Juanita, I add, "Allow me to enlighten you young ladies."

Taking a moment to rest my weary bones, I sit on a felled and charred tree trunk, then rest my shillelagh beside me and continue, "Dating back to ancient Rome, Agrippina poisoned her husband, the feeble yet quite brilliant Emperor Claudius, so that she could place her evil son, Nero on the throne. Agrippina attempted to rule Rome through her son, but misjudged him and paid the price." Adjusting my dentures and licking my dry lips, I continue, "Jumping forward, the bloody Hungarian Countess, Elizabeth Báthory, is regarded as one of the most prolific serial killers in history. Yet, we, too, had an American serial killer during the early twentieth century, named Belle Gunness, also known as the Butcher of Men. Lovely Belle lured forty victims into her Indiana Death Farm, and then slaughtered them like she did her pigs. She also murdered her two husbands and her innocent daughters." Taking a breath, I add, "And let's not forget Queen Bloody Mary, who found killing and burning Catholics quite cathartic."

Fighting for another breath of air to fill my laboring lungs, I finally exhale and glance at the two young gals before me, fixing my gaze on Juanita, hoping my lesson proves fruitful. "And one cannot forget the gruesome deeds of the women guards at Nazi death camps, like Irma Grese or Ilse Koch. For you see, they rose to the highest echelon of barbarism and sadistic evil ever perpetrated on this planet." Rubbing my wrinkled forehead, my mind recalls the horrific deeds as I almost shiver to say, "Ilse Koch, The Bitch of Buchenwald. She not only heartlessly teased and tortured hundreds of men, women, and children, but she decapitated some of them to make shrunken heads. And quite revoltingly, Ilse had also skinned many prisoners to make lampshades, as well as other bizarre *human-skinned* trinkets that she callously collected or sold to other degenerates." Gazing deeply into both of their eyes, I conclude, "So, don't kid yourselves, *kids*. Women *can* be monsters, too."

While Valery's face flinches with genuine distress, Juanita seems almost bored, as Adam unexpectedly says in a soft and melancholy voice, "I never mentioned this b-before, but my mother," he stutters, "attempted to k-kill me."

All of our heads snap in Adam's direction. Pensively, I rub my bristly chin as I readjust my dentures and swallow hard. Amid the uncomfortable silence, I query, "Are you serious?"

"Yes. Dead serious," Adam mutters. "Or should I say, *almost* dead. But, yes. Serious."

Valery shakes her head in disbelief. "Oh dear, Adam. That's horrible." She pauses only but a moment, and adds compassionately, "Why?"

Adam walks over to a twisted mound of rusted steel and somberly sits upon it. He gazes dejectedly at the ground and runs his hand along the edge of the crooked I-beam, a remnant not from a New Jersey building, but rather a gnarled girder from the Twin Towers at ground zero, which had been placed in Liberty Park as part of a heartrending 9/11 memorial. "My father died in nine-eleven," Adam utters, his voice uncharacteristically deep and sullen. "That was the beginning of my mother's decline. After that, well, she was never quite the same."

Juanita maneuvers closer to him, like a stealthy cougar sizing up its prey. "What's *that* got to do with you?"

Adam glances up, then dejectedly stares aimlessly at the ground once again. "She was ashamed of me." Tapping his slender piano fingers on the rusted memorial, he adds, "I just never measured up to her expectations."

Unfortunately, I knew what would transpire next. What had become quite evident over the past year was that Juanita rarely allowed tender emotions to seep through her Kevlar skin. With a twist of her lips, she says, "Well, screw her! She's dead now, Bucko. And you're like, one of four survivors now, right? So straighten up and let it go."

Adam closes his eyes and shakes his head as his shoulders droop like a sack of beans. Solemnly, he raises his eyes to glance at her, as if looking at another twisted piece of dense steel, and turns toward the mangled docks along the harbor. "You just wouldn't understand... I loved her."

Valery walks over and tenderly places her arm around him. "Back off, Juanita. He's right, you don't seem to understand a lot of things."

Unexpectedly, Juanita lunges at Valery, pulls her hair, and violently jostles her head back and forth, like a wild dog tearing into a piece of meat. Valery slips and falls awkwardly backward, her head smashing into a jagged edge of the rusted memorial. With a piercing shriek, Valery falls to the ground as blood gushes from the deep breach in her skull.

Adam rushes over and nervously lifts her head as I anxiously grasp my gnarled cane, trembling and unable to stand from the shock.

Valery winces in sheer pain as she gazes up at Juanita, while grasping her bloody scalp. "You bitch! You sick, evil bitch!" she spits.

Unsteadily, I manage to rise to my feet with the aid of my cane, rest it on my hip, and rip off one of my sleeves. I wrap it around Valery's head, but the river of blood saturates it instantly, coursing down her face and neck. Frantic, I glance around, foolishly looking for help, but the world population is just us four. Yet, the natural instinct to call for help when a task is not within your own capacity is a hard one to shake, as I stammer, "S-someone, p-please help her!" Catching my *faux pas*, I correct myself, "I m-mean, do either of you have any medical experience?"

Juanita heatedly crosses her arms and says cockily, "I wouldn't help that prissy bitch if my life depended on it."

Adam, despite his lanky frame, stands up with a

scowl and demands, "You *better* help her, you coldhearted bitch! I know you were an EMT. So help her, *now!*"

As Valery starts drifting into an unconscious state, I say, "Juanita, *please*, you must put your differences aside. For God's sake, Valery could very well die from that wound. Do something!"

Juanita rolls her eyes and twists her lips. "Look around, *amigos*! I have *no* equipment, *no* medications. Nothing. *Nada!* Zilch."

Adam snarls. "You mean to say you can't think of *anything* to do to help her? Where the hell did you learn your craft? At a flea-bag cantina in Mexico?"

Juanita steps aggressively toward Adam, who meekly recoils as she growls, "So, you wanna piece of me, pussy boy? Come on! Let's go!" As Adam stands mute, shaking like the Tin Man, Juanita continues, "I grew up in a house full of men, bucko, *real* men, not pansies, like you! So watch your step, peewee, before you end up like that spoiled, rich bitch. *Comprende?*"

Adam nervously bites his lips as he reaches down to feel Valery's pulse. "Oh, dear God! No! No!" he screeches. "She's dead!" Without even a twitch of remorse from Juanita, Adam anxiously looks at me.

Juanita sniggers with a snort just shy of an oink. "Ha! Why are you looking at that old windbag? That feeble ol' relic is as useless as you are, you pathetic wimp." Brashly, she marches up to Adam and antagonistically runs her fingers through his wavy, auburn hair. Gazing down at his jittery blue eyes, she says, "While all you can do is whine, my sweet little Chihuahua, all that prehistoric preacher can do is ramble on and on about his crappy generation and his long and boring life, a life already spent." Turning her menacing gaze on me, she adds, "And how fitting, that your world—ruled and *ruined* by men—will now start over again with a tough *chiquita* like *me*. The tide has turned, Papa."

Adam musters up a breath to respond. "Who the hell says we need you?"

Juanita laughs disdainfully as her head swivels back toward Adam. "You cowardly moron! In case you haven't noticed, *piñata* head, we three are the last humans on this planet, and you measly men need a superior woman to breed life." Peering deep into Adam's eyes, she says, "Unfortunately, this means I'll have to hookup with *you*, you pathetic worm." Turning her gaze at me, with twisted lips radiating revulsion, she adds, "Cause I sure as shit won't be caught dead shagging an old fart like *you!*"

My eyes suddenly widen with shock as I raise my hand. "*No!* Don't!"

The next vision I see is one of unimaginable horror as Adam strikes Juanita in the back of her head with a rusted piece of steel, splitting her head wide open.

"Dear God, no!" I yell again.

As Juanita falls to the ground, screaming in agony, Adam steps over her prostrate body, then nudges her onto her back with his makeshift weapon. It's a jarring image, reminiscent of Kubrick's killer ape wielding a deadly bone.

Juanita gazes up, shock marring her face, her eyes already bloodshot from the hammering blow. "You damn fool!" she snaps in devastating pain. "I'm the only chance you had to breed life again!" Glancing at me, she adds, "You see, your stupid species was destined to cause Armageddon." With a noxious sputter of blood and breath she spits, "Go fuck yourselves! 'Cause that's all you can do now w-without *me!*" Writhing in agony, she moans and mutters, "I'm g-glad it will end...w-with you two. P-path-e-tic...specccii... *men.*"

Adam peers down into her hateful eyes and says, "This world is better off without evil witches like *you*. And for your pea-brained information, we don't need you, you rat bitch. We *will* survive!"

With a last gurgle and a choke, Juanita let out a bellicose cackle, akin to the shrill of a dying hyena, and expires.

Meanwhile, I grasp my mouth in utter shock, my aged hand trembling uncontrollably. Standing in a hellish fog, stricken by the gruesome and profoundly disturbing chain of events—events that now have doomed mankind to the dustbin of extinction—I begin to weep.

Unsteadily, I lower myself onto a hunk of debris, remnants from the old train station that used to transport immigrants into the New World after being processed at Ellis Island. Realizing that this train station would certainly never run again, not for Americans, immigrants, nor any other human, my heart sinks. Closing my eyes, my feeble old head falls into the palms of my wrinkled hands, as tears bleed through my fingers, tears shed for the end of the human race.

Sobbing into the black abyss of my two hands—hands that signify the last two men on Earth—I suddenly feel another hand, one that tenderly pulls my hands away from my face and lifts my chin. Gazing up into Adam's now steadfast eyes, I blink in confusion. "You murdered not just a woman, Adam, but the entire human race."

Adam shakes his head ever so slightly. "You don't understand, Mr. Adams. She was wicked, and the new order of life on this planet shouldn't come from a monster like her."

A tormented giggle escapes from my nervous lips. In disbelief, I whimper, "Dear God, Adam. What in blazes are you thinking?" Gazing at Juanita and Valery's corpses, I say, "Our last two chances to start over again are gone." With a sob, I add, "We're finished. All of mankind is *finished*."

"No we're not," Adam says, seemingly without a trace of irony or insanity.

I gaze back up into his blue eyes and shake my head. "Adam, over the past year I have come to know that you are a very bright young man, with a compassionate heart. Yet, today you have bludgeoned to death not only a woman but also your own soul. The world, which we four had the last chance to revive, is now blackened by sin and total self-annihilation." With an unexpected wave of animus surging through me, my jaw tenses up as I scold, "Dear Lord, Adam! You committed *suicide*, suicide of the *human race*, damn you!"

An ironic smile sweeps across his handsome face. "Mr. Adams. You're an intelligent man. As you know, the Bible is full of seemingly wicked stories, as even the very beginning of mankind is full of murder and betrayal. Eve betrayed God's command and ate the apple, thrusting mankind into a world of sin. Juanita betrayed us and killed Valery." Pointing with a sense of relief at her corpse, he continues, "*She* was the murderer, Mr. Adams. She wouldn't even help Valery, all while knowing very well how to do so. I merely ended her evil reign among us, as many Jews and Christians have done to evildoers in the Bible or on the battlefields. What's more, do you recall Cain and Abel, Mr. Adams? To refresh your memory, *brother* killed *brother*."

With my anger subsiding, I gaze up at the clear blue sky, filled with pure white cumulus clouds. A soft breeze blows across my face as the smell of lilacs strangely titillates my nose, the purple flower being reproductively resilient, with fertile stamens and stigma in each flower. Out of nowhere, a dove gracefully flies by, then disappears. I shake my head and squint, not sure if what I just saw and smelled was an old man's whimsical illusion or a divine sign of new hope.

I gaze at Adam. "Yes, you're absolutely right, Adam. Betrayal, murder, and wickedness have all been a part of mankind from the very beginning. And even if you did kill an evil wretch with some justification, we are left with the disturbing fact that your act of ending evil has also catastrophically ended the human race."

To my utter confusion and frustration, Adam chuckles. Serious doubts about Adam's sanity grip me, as he says, "I know you are old, Mr. Adams, but I also know you are not deaf." Irritably, I gaze deep into his eyes, as he adds, "You did hear me say that we don't need her to start over, correct?"

I shake my head with a condescending snicker. "Adam, *your* name may be correct, but in case you haven't noticed, my name isn't Eve. Nor is my anatomy akin to hers. So, unless you know of a woman hiding somewhere, why are you making sick jokes at a profoundly disturbing time like this?"

Adam wipes his sweaty forehead as he speaks slowly, softly, reassuringly. "This certainly isn't a replay of Adam and Eve, Mr. Adams, but evidently we were chosen for a new order, one to be spawned by Adam and Adams."

"What the hell are you saying, Adam? Have you lost your mind?" Slowly, he begins to unbutton his shirt, as I say, "And just what the hell are you doing? I hope taking a swim in the Hudson to cool off."

Adam's slender fingers continue his striptease as he says, "As I eluded to before, Mr. Adams, I loved my mother dearly."

Nervously, I discreetly grasp my *cane*, wondering if I'll be *able* to use it. "Yes, and is this why she was ashamed of you? Because you're an exhibitionist or a pervert?"

Adam smiles, revealing his fine set of white teeth as he brushes the windswept hair away from his attractive face. "No, Mr. Adams. I'm no pervert. Once again, few stop to realize that mankind not only began with murder and betrayal, but also incest, of all things. Perhaps that's where all the world's problems originated, right in our defiled DNA. Who knows? But if you knew Turkish, you'd have known that my surname, Melez, means *hybrid* in English. You see, I'm a transgender, Mr. Adams. I was born with a uterus." Stopping his—rather, *her*—striptease and revealing a quasi-manly chest with small breasts, Adam adds, "Need I say more?"

Feverishly scratching my baldhead, I squint, as a deluge of thoughts barrage my senses, as if God was unleashing his devastating flood upon Noah inside my skull. And like Noah riding out the storm, I feel lost in time, as if for forty hellish days and forty surreal nights, until the mysterious tempest—with its blinding bolts of lightning and angry roars of thunder—finally begins to break and subside, my shock and bewilderment now confronting a new bizarre reality…and a new baffling decision.

Clasping my wrinkled hands in supplication, I gaze up to the heavens. "Dear Lord, is *this* your plan for a new dawn of mankind?"

My head falls as Adam sits beside me and compassionately wraps her arm around me, oddly bringing back memories of my childhood, as if being embraced and consoled simultaneously by my mother *and* father.

My mind reels. It seems the bizarre acts of murder and abnormal sex in Genesis—which ignited the procreation of mankind—are doomed to repeat themselves. Only this time with an even more peculiar twist.

Gazing up to the heavens, I cry, "Dear Lord! Will mankind, or *You*, ever learn?" Overcome with emotion, I passively yield and collapse into Adam's tender arms.

SPIRIT OF SORROW

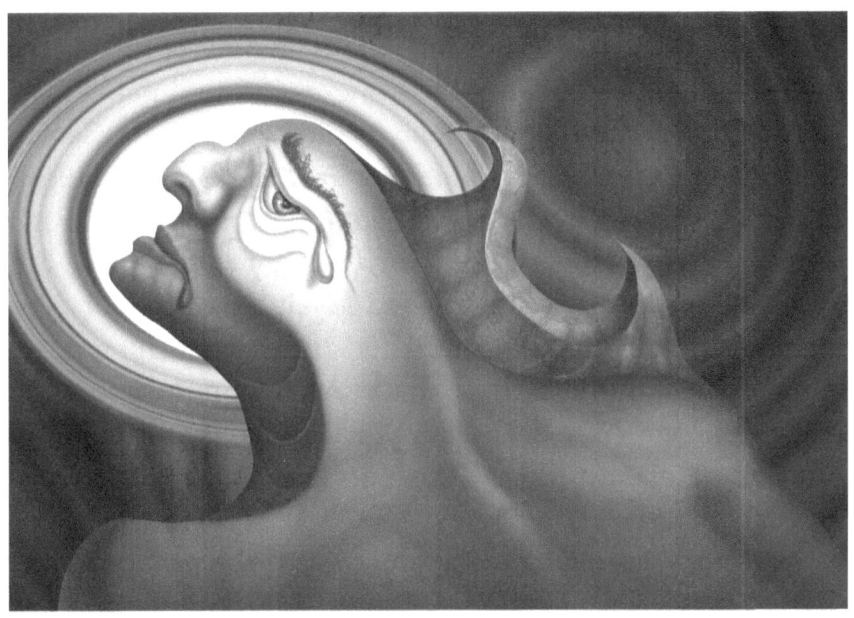

I spring up in bed, awake and sweating with my heart racing, all from a recurring dream that has plagued me for days. This mysterious figure, so lifelike, yet so vaporous, so surreal, yet somehow familiar, materializes out of the darkness of my tormented subconscious. The face is haunting, sad, with penetrating eyes that dig into my heart and twist it of its last drops of blood. Yet not in malice, but with an unknown agenda that rings the deepest emotions of empathy and compassion out of my tortured soul, so much so that I have often awakened with tears in my eyes, akin to those in his, whom I call the Spirit of Sorrow.

This quasi-humanoid, alien phantom—with a scalloped mane and gill-like slits on its neck—bears an ever so slight resemblance to an American Indian. But perhaps that's merely a superficial illusion, based upon my earthly dedication to justice and humanitarian efforts.

You see, my name is Armstrong—not like Neil Armstrong, the great American hero who first set foot on the moon. Rather, I adopted Armstrong as my first name from one of my childhood idols, namely General George Armstrong Custer. As a young boy growing up in the 1960s, I, like most boys my age, was enthralled with the Custer legend. He was the tragic war hero who captured our imaginations through bravery and loyalty to his nation. Yet, it's hard to deny that it was Custer's heart-wrenching death at the Battle of Little Bighorn that stuck in our guts most and made us love him even more. Facing a vastly superior number of enemy forces, Custer's last stand was indeed inevitable.

Moreover, that Errol Flynn played the part of Custer in the 1941 film, *They Died With Their Boots On*, surely enhanced many a young boy's desire to grow up to be just like him, minus his brutal finale. Yet, Errol had also been a critical factor in conjuring up some misconceptions, as Errol was stunningly handsome and irresistibly charismatic, especially to women, many of whom he made starry-eyed and weak-kneed. Whereas Custer may have had charisma, he was no Errol Flynn.

But then seasons passed as years rolled into decades, and the scribes took to revising the history books. The hero had morphed into the anti-hero, just like Andrew Jackson and others, as confusion and bittersweet thoughts clouded the minds of many Americans. Meanwhile, the youngsters of today, never having learned the other side, view Custer with repugnance in their hearts, as if they likewise had morphed into descendants of the Sioux and Cheyenne tribes, harboring an intense loathing for the aggressive European races. Certainly, Custer was no angel, as the primary sources that have come to the fore paint a clearer picture, undoubtedly one far different and sobering than Hollywood's dramatized depiction.

Despite Custer's many faults that deserve censure, he was just a warrior, following orders and defending his way of life, just as the Sioux and Cheyenne were defending theirs. His kin, while also engaging in deceit, had superior weapons and more sophisticated technologies that enabled his race to prevail. For the notion that Native Americans were peaceful Plains people who never warred or slaughtered their enemies is just as false and fanciful as Hollywood's fictitious movies.

The horrific mutilations and brutal act of scalping—of cutting or ripping off an enemy's scalp while dead or alive, which bloodied the battlefields—were not techniques invented by the white man, nor was the brutal act of allowing tribal women and boys to strip Custer and his men naked and then beat many of their skulls to gooey pulp with stone-headed clubs, while also savagely hacking their genitals and body parts. What's more, Rain-in-the-Face carved out the heart of Custer's brother Tom, and, in a ferocious frenzy, bit into it. Nor must we forget the disturbing Carib native tribe, being cannibals who viciously slaughtered and ate enemy tribesmen and Europeans.

The bottom line is, savagery unfortunately resides in the breasts of all races. And in the case of Custer and the American Natives, both had acted like animals, and one animal won.

Yet, I digress. What am I to make of this tormenting apparition, this strange Spirit of Sorrow who haunts me? Does it wish to punish me for my views? After all, I no longer hold the same reverence for Custer as I once did.

What's more, I must make clear that I am a prominent defender of human rights, having been called the National Organizing Humanitarian/Ambassador of True Equality, or N.O. H.A.T.E.

You see, I vigorously defend the true underdogs, the overlooked minorities who lack the large and powerful representation that some minority groups possess. Therefore, I cater mostly to the Polish, Lithuanians, Czechs, Croatians, Middle Easterners, and other underrepresented groups, many of whom don't even speak English or Spanish. They are the truly forgotten souls; the ones in desperate need of assistance. And despite my continued, yet tarnished, respect for Custer, I have become a true egalitarian and defender of the American Indian, or Native American as they wish to be called, for I truly seek amends and righteous equality for this forgotten race that had almost faced extinction. While other races have faced hardship, prejudice, and malice, this race had almost been eradicated off the face of the Earth.

That said, being one of the nation's leading humanitarians, this all the more brings me back to my dilemma, this incessant nightmare that dominates my slumber and saturates my waking thoughts, for I long for answers.

Is it my empathy for this race that explains this strange apparition's slightly Native American features?

I don't know.

Or perhaps that familiar imagery is there to derail my thoughts and shield its true evil intentions.

Again, I'm not sure.

All I do know is that this alien spirit lurks in my mind—it consumes me. But what, dear Lord, is its mission? Its intent? Is it to enlighten, or simply frighten me?

Once again, the clock strikes twelve, as my eyes grow weary. My trepidation of falling asleep has grown as disturbing as the dream itself, as I sit upright in bed and fight to stay awake. Eager to divert my attention, I open a book of humorous short stories, hoping they'll obliterate my sorrowful dream with laughter. As I read the pages, and giggle once or twice, the lamp on my night table flickers. Perhaps it's just an old bulb or a power surge, yet I find the flicker disturbing. It interrupts my joyful read and irritates my sensitive eyes. Removing my glasses to massage my eyes, I then place the glasses back on, only to see the light flicker once again, this time erratically until, finally, it *pops*! With a jolt, I blink hard, as the room goes black.

My head spins amid the abyss, seeking the slightest glimmer of light. But I see nothing. My luck, the sun and moon happen to be in the same ecliptic longitude, thus causing a new moon—and total darkness. Unable to see the book before me, or even my hand, I place the book down on the bed. Yet before I even attempt to set my foot on the floor, a dark, bluish glow begins to illuminate the room, ever so slightly. The eerie blue light reveals a startling occurrence as it morphs into a semi-solid facade of swirling blue waves, made up of molecular rings that begin twisting and contorting into odd shapes. Out of this swirling wall appears a small white dot, which slowly telescopes in size toward me, revealing what appears to be a large oval window or tunnel. I can't be sure, as I frantically remove my glasses, wipe them clean with my undershirt, and hurriedly place them back on.

Now trembling, my heart races as a mysterious vapor emerges from the luminous white tunnel, materializing into the haunting phantom of my dreams: the Spirit of Sorrow. Blinking hard, with sweat moistening my brow, I struggle to make sense of this weird alien that continues to invade my worlds, of both sleep and now reality. The Spirit, once again, gazes at me with his deep blue eyeball, only this time it is no illusion, but frighteningly real, as is the tangible teardrop that slips over its eyelid and falls to my bedroom floor. From the corner of its mouth, a drop of blood oozes down its chin, as the alien life form begins to recede into the glowing tunnel of light, beckoning me with a subtle wave of its hand.

As fear turns to intrigue, I find myself rising out of bed, slipping on clothes and following the alien, as I walk past the blue swirling walls and climb into the bright tunnel. As if in an elevator made of pure light, the Spirit and I seem to merge with the light and traverse space and time, of what I can only imagine must be many light-years away, into a far-off galaxy or distant quadrant of the universe. Within minutes, however, we land on a strange and eerie planet.

There before me is an alien race, revolting creatures that send a shiver down my spine. Perhaps the closest description I can venture to say would be the combination of a deep-sea angler fish with a vampire squid; the angler feature being its ugly, hideous head and the squid's red, rubbery, bat-like webbing attached between its two arms and body, as well as between its four legs, giving the creature an almost red, umbrella-like skirt. As speculated, the Spirit of Sorrow's faint American Indian features now begin to morph right before my eyes into one of these atrocious-looking creatures.

Although I'm unable to communicate with them, I find myself mysteriously drawn along by their thoughts, as if by telepathy. Suddenly, I sense why the Spirit had visited my dreams. It was to acclimate me to its odd presence, so when it did finally materialize, I would be less fearful—which, oddly enough, I am now, as it gazes at me with its large, fish-like eyes and beckons me with its tentacle arm.

As I begin to follow the Spirit, and his entourage of fellow creatures, I start to notice more perceptively the peculiar terrain of their planet. Unlike Earth, their terrain is pliable and in constant flux, as if a huge, taut waterbed. But rather than smooth plastic, the planet's skin is textured, and quite rocky. In the distance, I can see colorful meadows glistening under the planet's three suns, and beyond that, towering spiked mountains of various hues, like gargantuan stalagmites, which surround large lakes or perhaps seas, boiling with a metallic, golden lava, as vapor rises from the smoldering sludge.

Struggling to maintain my balance on the shifting terrain, I still manage to keep up with their brisk pace. Oddly enough, as we journey, I find myself becoming not only very comfortable with their weird looks, but feel a growing, natural bond with them, an almost innate connection that's hard to describe. I assume that their DNA, if they have any, is nothing like ours, yet if there is some sort of molecular kinship between our species, I feel it.

As we march along, several creatures exchange hand signals with me as we manage to bond further. Scanning the group, I notice how some aliens have babies latched onto their backs in translucent pouches, each at various stages of development, and each connected by an umbilical cord. Seeing that these fleshy pouches have dissolved on other females, it's clear that their reproductive process occurs outside their bodies, making birth significantly easier for the female of the species.

Glancing around, I notice that among the predominantly congenial pack, several male aliens furtively whisper something discordant, then gaze at me with evil eyes, as the entourage begins to mount a formation at the edge of a precipice. As the caravan comes to a stop, the male aliens spread open their webbed flesh to reveal what appears to be a harpoon-like gun.

A wave of confusion and tension comes over me as the leader, or Spirit of Sorrow, approaches me. Morphing back into the slightly American Indian-like figure, he finally speaks. However, it is a cacophony of gibberish, akin to a cross between a whale call and a wild monkey's screech.

Shaking my head to signal that I don't understand, he resorts to hand gestures, pointing to a large monolith, which I can only describe as a monument with graphic etchings. As I near the colossal structure I see what appears to be hieroglyphs, perhaps detailing their history. As my eyes scan the etchings of various symbols and drawings—of what I imagine are prominent members of their past—they land on an image that startles me. It's a crude and gruesome depiction of a battle scene, where these creatures are cutting off the heads of their enemies and eating them. The next image in line shows the victors with larger, exaggerated heads, evidently gaining greater mental acuity from the devoured heads of the fallen, or at least I presume that's their belief. The next image in line portrays a peaceful village populated with the Spirit's clan, being illuminated by the planet's three venerated suns.

The Spirit of Sorrow points to that image, gazes at me with a solemn expression, then points to the edge of the cliff, where a platoon of his warriors stand ready. Yet as we approach the edge, the shoreline below reveals a jarring sight. Affixing my glasses to reassure my mind of what I'm seeing, I lose my footing as my knees quiver with fear and bewilderment. At the bottom of this two-thousand-foot cliff, I see a vast ocean. On the shoreline are hundreds of spaceships, with thousands of ant-like creatures crawling out of them. However, they are not ants at all. They're full-scale invaders. The warriors around me point to their battling kin below who are fighting desperately for their lives.

Confused as to why they chose *me* to view this horrific battle, or what I could possibly do, the Spirit of Sorrow hands me a steampunk-style device, which evidently is a primitive form of binoculars. Removing my glasses, I grasp it and gaze down into the squall of battle.

I almost drop them as my heart stalls. On the spaceship, I see the unmistakable flag of the United States! As I scan the area, I see humans with laser-powered weapons mowing down swaths of the Spirit's fellow creatures, who are fighting a futile battle with their crude spear guns.

Suddenly, the reason the Spirit brought me here, and his American Indian visage, hits me like a tomahawk. I lower the field glasses to gaze at the Spirit, then, still not believing my eyes, I peer into them once again, only to see the same American assault. It's unimaginable, but now very clear. I had traveled not only through space but also time, as these American soldiers below are from the future. Again, I lower the binoculars and gaze at the Spirit of Sorrow, who points at me, then down at the carnage below. His message is clear, and I now know why I was chosen.

Descending the precarious cliff with a platoon trailing behind, I eventually approach the battlefield, as spears whiz past my head from behind and beams of deadly lasers dismember or incinerate scores of creatures before me.

Meanwhile, sporting red and blue uniforms with white helmets and dark goggles, the humans continue to annihilate the creatures en masse, when one of the human soldiers spots me. Waving for me to fall behind their lines into safety, I shake my head and wave my hands, signaling, *NO! STOP!*

No sooner do I wave, than a spear impales me from behind, entering my back and blowing blood and guts out from my chest. In agony, I fall forward, prostrate on the ground.

Suddenly, the creatures cease fighting, evidently receiving a telepathic signal from the Spirit, who gazes angrily at one of his warriors, then approaches me and pulls the spear out of my back. Flipping me over, tears drip down from his eyes as he caresses my head tenderly, lovingly.

As my eyes roll up to his mournful face, I clasp his arm affectionately. Whether the arrow was intentional or not no longer matters. As silence and confusion envelops the battlefield, I gaze up at the approaching human warriors and say, "These are my friends. *Please*, stop the killing." As blood oozes out of my mouth and tears of pain leak out of my eyes, I add, "Why? Why are you killing them?"

As the U.S. soldiers fix their weapons on the creatures, the leader removes his helmet and peers down at me, equally confused. "Who the hell are you? And how did you get here?"

"I'm Armstrong." Pointing at the Spirit I continue, "The Spirit beckoned me here to end this madness." With a grunt of pain, I repeat, "Why are you killing them?"

The commander smirks. "Surely you must know, Armstrong," he says with irritation as he turns his gaze at his enemy. "This Spirit, as you call him, whom *we* call Azzendor, and his Azzen tribe initially welcomed us here, because Earth's climate has become extremely hostile and untenable. Not to mention the man-made toxins that have polluted the air, water, and our processed foods. Earthlings are on transports as we speak, and should arrive in five years time. So, you know darn well our very survival depends on making a settlement here, Armstrong. Yet they have already brutally decapitated many of our women and even children, and…" Staring at the Spirit with hate in his eyes, he snaps, "They *ate* them! They're savages!"

I raise my hand. "Hold on! First of all, I'm not from your time. I'm from the year 2018. So I *don't* know how bad things have gotten on Earth."

The commander squints and shakes his head. "Come off it, Armstrong. We, in the twenty-third century, have mastered space travel, but *time*? Sorry, not buying it."

As I maintain firm pressure on my bleeding wound, I say, "Well, I assure you that I did in fact travel through time, through some type of electro-bio-fusion tunnel or wormhole. How else could I get here?" Managing to pull my wallet out of my pocket, I slip out my driver's license and raise it up, to the commander's surprise.

He practically ignores the date and says, "Is that to drive a fossil-fueled automobile? I've only seen those in old holograms back at the academy."

"Yes," I say with a grunt. "I figured mankind would have eventually done away with them."

The commander turns and waves to a fellow soldier, who approaches me with a white case and opens it. As he assembles an odd contraption, he says, "Then I guess you don't know what this is, right?"

"Not a clue," I utter in pain. "But I hope it's something to seal up this wound."

"Indeed it is, Armstrong. It will not only heal the superficial wound, but will also repair any internal organs that were damaged. And I have an eZ-mender that will even repair your bloody shirt, making it like new again."

As he waves the device over my wounds, they practically disappear, leaving only a blemish behind. Then with a wave of the eZ-mender, my shirt miraculously mends before my eyes, as the bloody stains dissolve.

I thank the medic and gaze up at the commander. "I thank you, as well. I'm happy to see that mankind continues to make great strides in progress. Your spaceship and these devices are quite impressive." As the commander and medic both nod with a smile, I sit upright and add, "Yet, I must ask, why hasn't mankind progressed in the fields of compassion or attaining true justice?"

As their smiles morph into smirks, the commander replies, "As I told you, Armstrong, these savages started the killings. And worse yet, their barbaric cannibalism even robbed me of my own two sons." Fighting to hold back tears of rage, he continues, "Although I just follow orders, and try not to make this war personal, I cannot forgive that butchery! They're head-eating parasites!" Turning his gaze to the Spirit, he begins to bellow in a whale-like screech with unnerving overtones, akin to a wild boar. The bone-chilling diatribe escalates as the Spirit responds in kind.

With my wound and pain fully abated, I stand up, as their verbal assaults finally cease. I glance at the Spirit, then firmly at the commander. "You speak their language?"

"Of course. It took the several months that we've been here to grasp it, but yes. Many of us can speak to these animals!"

Not wishing to see another genocide or another gory last stand, I say, "I might as well tell you, commander, that I'm an official Ambassador of Justice. And as an American, I trust you'll listen to my counsel."

The commander squints. "Wait a minute. You said you're from 2018? You're not *the* Armstrong who founded the global organization N.O. H.A.T.E., are you?"

A smile sweeps across my face. "Jesus, you mean to say it survived?"

The commander's stern face took on a look of profound admiration. "Hell, yeah! I mean, yes, sir. My mother is very active in your organization. In fact, you're her idol."

I actually blush. "In that case, please heed the noble wishes of your mother and my request." Glancing at the Spirit, I add, "Commander, can you please ask him to tell us *why* they committed those atrocities?"

With some hesitation and a huff, the commander says, "It's only because of who you are that I'll entertain this, sir," as he turns and squeals the question in Azzenese.

Receiving the Spirit's discordant reply, the commander turns back toward me and says, "He claims we had mistreated and killed their kind. However, let me make this clear. While it is true that a handful of our early settlers ran roughshod over these primitive creatures, and did commit some unthinkable acts, they were *not* the majority. As you must know, every race or species has a small percentage of bad apples. It's akin to how a few crimes by a handful of belligerent fools cause new laws to be enacted, laws that are often times far too severe and unjust for the vast majority. Yet all suffer for the sins of a few."

Putting my arm around the Spirit's broad shoulders, I say, "Well, knowing that, isn't it time that humankind learns from its mistakes? Why must centuries or millennia pass before logic, compassion, and a sense of *true* justice can prevail? If only mankind's heart and soul would advance in unison with its mental capacity for innovation and progress, we could truly claim to be just and admirable creatures." Glancing at the Spirit, I add, "And a few of these creatures have made horrible mistakes, as well—one very likely harpooning *me*. So before you engage in another genocide, please, I beg you both to work this out peacefully."

The commander's stern gaze veers toward the Spirit, then back at me, as he says, "But what about my—"

"Your sons cannot be brought back to life," I interject, knowing that personal tragedy often incites a rash response. "We must temper our actions, commander, as I learned from history, when President McKinley was shot. His response wasn't 'shoot the bastard!' It was 'go easy on him, boys,' as his security team apprehended the assassin." With that, the commander solemnly lowers his head and sighs.

"Furthermore, these savage creatures, which you call them, may live crude and simple lives, but they somehow managed to figure out how to traverse not only space but also *time*. Moreover, we arrived here from Earth in the matter of minutes, not five years. So there is much both races can learn from each other."

The commander's head rises with intrigue. Asking a battery of questions, we discuss at length my fantastical journey, then my official endeavors, which are ongoing for me, but historical occurrences for him. He then returns to the topic of the aliens, their monuments, traits, and knowledge of time travel. On the conclusion of our talks the commander finally lowers his weapon, impressed by the Azzen's various, and hitherto unknown, abilities. Turning about, he orders his men to stand down, then looks back at the Spirit. The two engage in a lengthy discordant dialogue, which eventually ends with the former combatants peacefully collecting their fallen warriors and making arrangements to begin their relationship anew, in peace.

The Spirit issues, what appear to be, commands to his fellow creatures, then approaches me and humbly bows his head. Extending his arms, I walk contentedly into his warm embrace. Then with a tender nod and graceful smile, the Spirit of Sorrow becomes, what I now call, the Spirit of Joy.

However, with his shape-change no longer necessary, the Spirit once again resumes his natural form. Despite his angler fish-like head and vampire squid arms and legs, I have somehow grown accustomed to their appearance, and no longer have the slight chills I once had. And in all honesty, although I still cannot call them handsome or beautiful by my own ingrained standards, they are amazing creatures, with handsome and beautiful dispositions.

Be that as it may, the bittersweet thought of returning home not only strikes me, but also my dear new friend, whose strange fish-like eyes gaze at me, then veer back in the direction of the bioelectric wormhole of time and space. I nod my consent, as his stiff, bony jaw manages to twist into a sad expression of loss.

I turn and say goodbye to the commander, his medic, and the unit, as the Spirit grasps my hand with his tentacle and escorts me back to the transporter. As we approach the white, oval tunnel, I point at the Spirit, then at my chest, and finally into the glowing void. Yet, he shakes his head. *No.* This time I will have to travel alone. With the Spirit's telekinetic blink, the luminous wormhole enlarges as he points to it. It's time—time to go back in time.

Again, we embrace, only this time I'm enveloped by his two arms and two of his four legs. The warm and titillating touch of his rubbery appendages reverberate throughout my body, solidifying the bond of friendship we share, which is oddly overwhelming, deep, and emotional, as a tear wells in his eye, along with one in mine. Offering each other amicable nods, we part, as I climb into the electro-luminous wormhole, and within a few minutes of merging with the light, I arrive back in my bedroom.

Gazing around at my lovely room, with its array of photographs on the dresser of my wife and children, then over at my soft, comfortable bed, with my book of humorous short stories still on it, I laugh with relief.

My laughter alerts my wife, who strolls buoyantly in. "What's so funny? And who else is in here?"

"No one, sweetheart, but it's great to see you!"

Her eyebrows pinch with suspicion. "Now I know something's up. What is it?"

I chuckle again. "Actually, you won't believe me, dear."

"Try me."

"Okay," I say, "I just traveled into the future, to a distant planet, where I stopped mankind from annihilating the native Azzen creatures. And—"

"All right, that's enough." Gazing at the book on the bed, she adds, "I see you're in a giddy mood, Armstrong." As she slips into her nightgown and then into bed, she picks up the book of humorous stories and smirks. "So is this alien nonsense of yours from a silly tale in this book?"

"No, honestly," I say with a deadpan face. "I'm serious, sweetheart. In fact, do you remember that recurring dream I've mentioned, you know, the haunting Spirit of Sorrow? Well, he's real."

"And you're really scaring me, Armstrong. Stop it. It's not funny. Now just get into bed and shut off the light. It's late."

"Ah, yes, the light! Didn't you see the lights flicker and go out before?"

"Yes, yes, we had a brief power outage. That's it. No visitors from outer space, I'm sad to say. Now, *please*, get into bed and shut the light!" she says with more annoyance.

"Okay, have it your way. But in reality, it doesn't matter if anyone here on Earth believes me, I know I saved an alien race and aided mankind's very future."

My wife rolls her eyes. "Please, just come *back to reality* and back to bed!"

As I remove my shirt, a thought strikes me. "Okay, so how do you explain this?" I say, as I lift my undershirt and point to the blemish where the spear had pierced me.

"Darling, that's from the skin cancer ablation you had last month. Now come on, end this childish nonsense. My God," she huffs, exasperated, "men certainly have a different sense of humor than women!" With that, she throws my book of humor on the floor.

Dumbfounded, I lay in bed and shut off the light, wondering.

Thank You

To all the great sources of inspiration, from novelists to nonfiction and from all the other sources of media that have fed my imagination, including the genius of Rod Serling and his fellow writers in the Zone, I thank you!

A special thanks also goes to *some* of my favorite rock groups: namely Blue Oyster Cult, Black Sabbath, and Pink Floyd, as snippets of their lyrics were featured in *Life of a Shyster*. While lyrics of The Four Seasons appeared in *The Helicon*. Their music has been a part of my life, as it has for millions of others, so I was honored to incorporate them as a small token of my gratitude.

To my steadfast family and friends, and of course my dear readers, who have supported my creative endeavors, along with my editors, marketers and to all the international contest judges who have voted several of my books as award winners, I am most grateful. *Thank you!*

— Rich DiSilvio

My Nazi Nemesis

GOLD AWARD WINNER

★★★★★ **"DiSilvio's plot is cunning and ingenious!"**
-- Jack Magnus for Readers' Favorite

A deadly love triangle launches a father and daughter team to hunt down a nefarious Nazi. Yet twists and turns abound, leading to a shocking climax.

Hardcover: 9780981762586
Paperback: 9780981762579
eBook: 9780981762593

A Blazing Gilded Age

INTERNATIONAL AWARD WINNER

A riveting rags-to-riches saga about a poor family's struggle to survive amid a nation burning with ambition yet bleeding with injustice. Features, Teddy Roosevelt, JP Morgan, Mark Twain, Tesla and more.

Lauded by HISTORY/A+E and noted biographer Roger DiSilvestro.

Hardcover: 9780981762562
Paperback: 9780981762555
eBook: 9780997680720

Tales of Titans Series

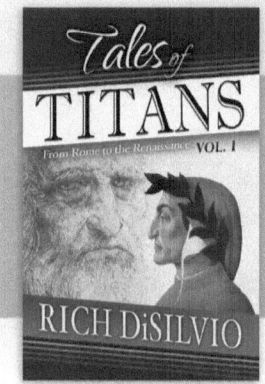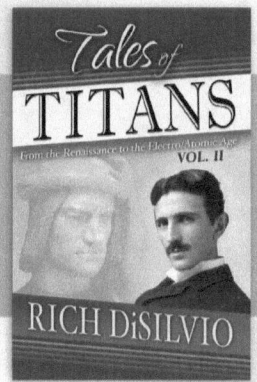

Tales of Titans brings great historical figures to life with concise yet compelling essays, coupled with engaging narratives that enlighten readers to their miraculous deeds, and misdeeds, that have significantly shaped Western civilization.

This handsomely illustrated series offers readers brief biographical overviews and cogent analysis, while the quasi-fictional scenarios transport readers into a fascinating past, whereby putting flesh on the bones of several titans and offering glimpses into their hearts, minds, and actions.

Tales of Titans, Vol. I : From Rome to the Renaissance
Augustus & Livia, Vespasian & Titus, Hadrian, Constantine, Dante, Brunelleschi, Columbus, Vespucci, King Ferdinand, Pope Alexander VI & Cesare Borgia, and Leonardo da Vinci.

Tales of Titans, Vol. II: Renaissance to the Electro/Atomic Age
The Medicis, Gutenberg, Lorenzo de Medici, Savonarola, Leonardo & Machiavelli, Martin Luther, Queen Elizabeth I, Shakespeare, Galileo, Darwin, Marx, Stalin, Freud, Marconi, Edison, Tesla, Westinghouse, Einstein, Fermi and von Braun.

Tales of Titans, Vol. III: Founding Fathers, Women Warriors & WWII
Samuel Adams, Thomas Paine, George Washington, John Adams, Thomas Jefferson, James Madison, Alexander Hamilton, Ben Franklin, Sybil Ludington, James Armistead Lafayette, Elizabeth Cady Stanton, Susan B. Anthony, Harriet Tubman, Adolf Hitler, FDR & Churchill

Liszt's *Dante Symphony*

A historical mystery/thriller highlighting the belligerent rise of Nazi Germany from its Prussian roots, replete with ciphers, spies, murder and a stellar cast, including Albert Einstein, Rossini, Liszt, Nazi officers and Adolf Hitler.

Hardcover: 9780981762548
Paperback: 9780981762531
eBook: 9780997680713

The Winds of Time

The Winds of Time is a historical tour de force of Western civilization by Rich DiSilvio.

With masterful style, DiSilvio paints a fascinating historical canvas with the flare of a consummate artist. Key figures and the primary cultures that literally shaped the Western world are candidly analyzed, revealing both the dark and luminous sides of mankind. Moreover, DiSilvio's insightful essays add intriguing new dimensions to the historical record.

Hardcover: 9780981762524
eBook: 9780997680706

FIRST PLACE WINNER

Meet My Famous Friends

Inspiring kids with Humor!
A whimsical picture book that pays homage to great historical figures in imaginative ways.

Author/Illustrator Rich DiSilvio presents a broad array of geniuses and heroes in a humorous and compelling fashion by altering their names and appearances, whereby making us see very familiar people in very different ways.

While children will get a kick out of looking at the comical artwork, teens and even adults will appreciate the witty play on words, inventive creations, and perhaps glean a thing or two about some of these iconic people who had a great influence on society in one form or another. Their lives and contributions have uplifted humanity in various ways, thus being great role models for young and old alike.

Hardcover: 9780997680751 Paperback: 9780997680768 eBook: 9780997680775

PURPLE DRAGONFLY WINNER

Danny and the DreamWeaver

A MS novelette by Mark Poe (aka Rich DiSilvio) about the power of dreams and the imagination.

When Danny meets Nostrildamus in his dream a bizarre journey begins!

Packed with dry humor, a mystery, and zany-looking artists, like Michelanjello & Hippopotamus Bosch, *Danny and the DreamWeaver* is an imaginative adventure of criminal intrigue and art history that demonstrates the importance of looking at life differently.

Paperback: 9780997680737
eBook: 9780997680744

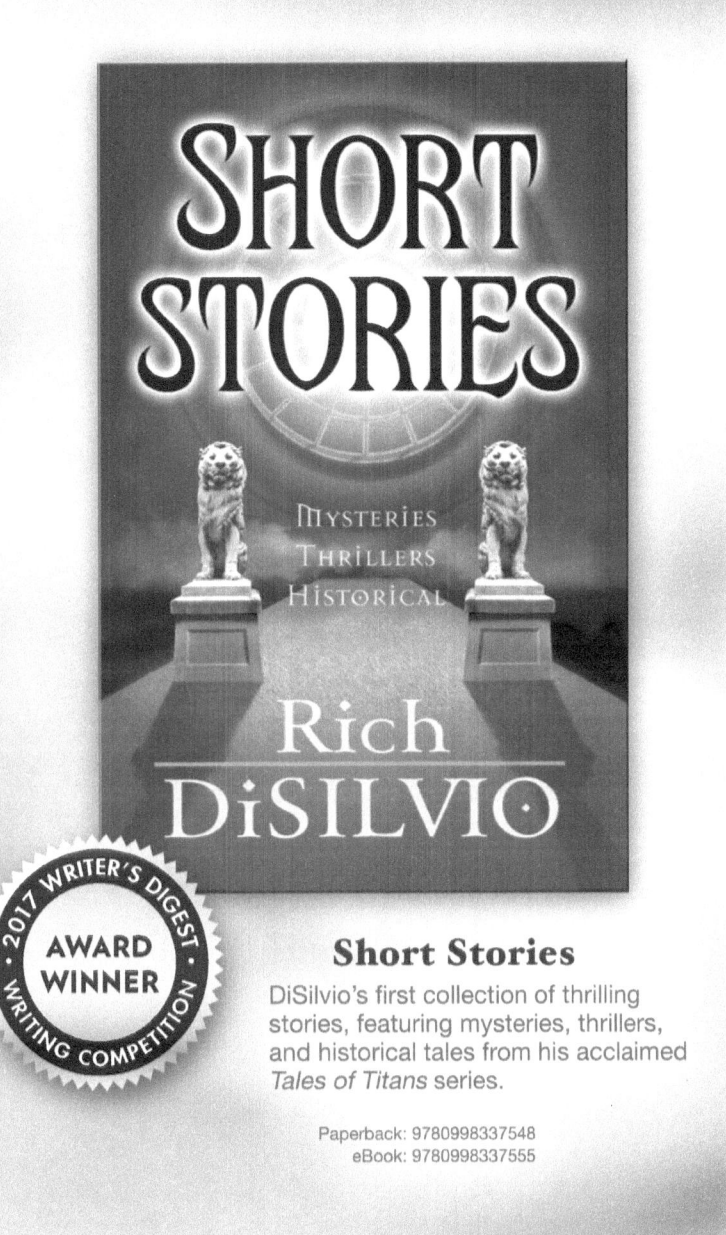

Short Stories

DiSilvio's first collection of thrilling stories, featuring mysteries, thrillers, and historical tales from his acclaimed *Tales of Titans* series.

Paperback: 9780998337548
eBook: 9780998337555

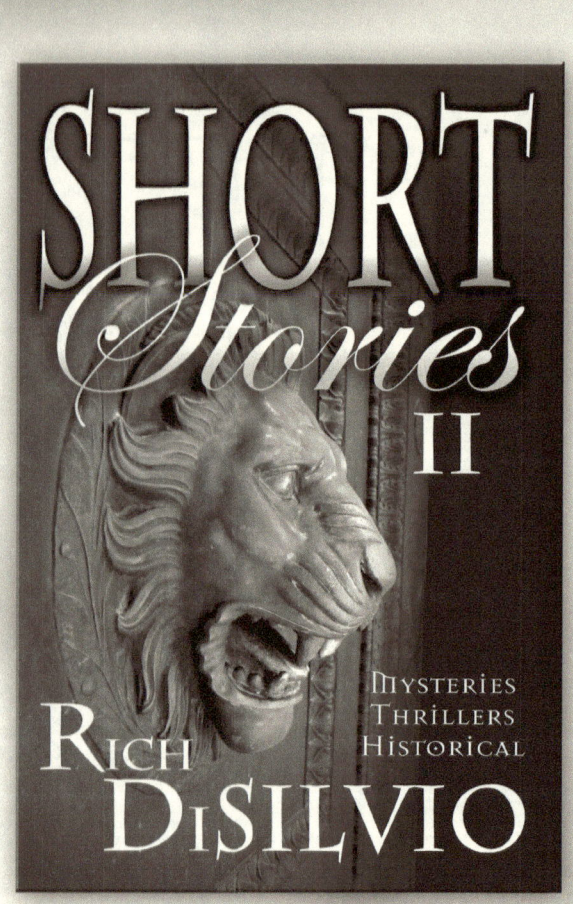

Short Stories II

DiSilvio's second collection of thrilling
stories, featuring mysteries, thrillers,
and historical tales from his acclaimed
Tales of Titans series.

Paperback: 9780998337562
eBook: 9780998337579

www.ingramcontent.com/pod-product-compliance
Lightning Source LLC
Chambersburg PA
CBHW031128210626
46816CB00015B/1184